The bell rings.

"Bye, Harrison," I say. He stands, gathers up his things. I stand too. He faces me, slinging his bag over his left shoulder.

He repeats, "Harrison," putting extra emphasis on rolling the *rr*'s. Trying to pronounce it like I did. He can't do it. That's another thing I've noticed about English: no double *rr*'s. "Say it again," he says.

"Harrison."

"First you teach me math, then you make my name beautiful."

I smile as I zip my bag. *Your name is beautiful*, I think, but is another thing I do not say.

LOVE in ENGLISH

Maria E. Andreu

BALZER + BRAY

An Imprint of HarperCollins*Publishers*

Balzer + Bray is an imprint of HarperCollins Publishers.

Love in English
Copyright © 2021 by Alloy Entertainment and Maria E. Andreu
All rights reserved. Printed in the United States of America.
No part of this book may be used or reproduced in any manner whatsoever
without written permission except in the case of brief quotations
embodied in critical articles and reviews.
For information address HarperCollins Children's Books, a division of
HarperCollins Publishers, 195 Broadway, New York, NY 10007.
www.epicreads.com

Library of Congress Control Number: 2020943927
ISBN 978-0-06-299652-7

Typography by Jenna Stempel-Lobell
23 24 25 26 27 LBC 6 5 4 3 2
❖
First paperback edition, 2022

For everyone who has ever strained to find the words:
I hear you

YOUR FUTURE DEPENDS ON UNDERSTANDING THIS

Primero, lee todas las instrucciones. No te olvides de llegar hasta el final.

(Si crees que final es una palabra que entiendes, algún tipo de pista, estás equivocada.)

Las instrucciones son así: Escucha a todos, aprende todo, mantente al día, no extrañes nada. Y hazlo todo en un idioma que no entiendes.

¿Sí?

Okay. Let's begin.

THE FIRST DAY

I smooth the front of my skirt, then run a finger on the checked gray felt of the front seat of the car. My toes are cold in my boots even though it is not cold out. I wasn't nervous this morning getting ready. But now I feel locked in. Like: This is the outfit. This is the day. This is the me that does it, not some imaginary future me.

My dad studies my face and hands me a box of Tic Tacs, the base of his left hand on the steering wheel, like he's bracing himself. Tic Tacs. Our old before-school routine since I was little. If there was a reason once, I've forgotten it now. I shouldn't be surprised that there are Tic Tacs here, but I am. Their rattle feels like it comes from far away. I pop one in my mouth. I hand the box back.

Everything has been strange in the two weeks since my mom and I got to this new country. To our new home in New Jersey, on Eighty-Fifth Street in a small town. It is a place that hasn't decided if it wants to grow up to be a farm or a strip mall. Everything is green and pushy here, insisting on itself. The landscape is not scrappy like it is back home in Argentina. My mom listens to the radio in Spanish, but it's not the Spanish we speak. Cashiers always seem to be in such a hurry, like they're paid by the customer. Another strange thing: we drive everywhere, moving from bubble to bubble—from our dingy new apartment to the car to the store and back. And now this school.

I sit and look at the building's unfriendly brick face. My father's eyes watch me.

"You will be okay, Ana," he says in English. He insists that my family only speak English so we can learn it faster. "You just have to get through the first day."

That's not true and he knows it. Today is the first of more days than I can count.

He continues, "Everyone will want to know who the new student is."

I still do not look his way.

"It's our new adventure," he says in a tone that begs me to agree.

I look at him, finally. It is still jarring, this new father of mine, three years older than the one who last lived with me. His face is rounder. The battalion at the front lines of his head has lost several rows of troops to the Balding Brigade. We used to Skype with him all the time when my mom and I were back home and he was here, but it's different in person. Everything is different in person.

Suddenly, I want to cry. I did not ask for this adventure. But as soon as I think that, I feel guilty. I close my eyes and remember my cousins back home telling me how lucky I am. And I *am* lucky.

But today I don't feel lucky at all.

Los números

19,000,000: The number of people who apply for the U.S.A Diversity Visa Program each year.

Less than 1%: Immigrants who get a Green Card.

17: Times my father entered the immigration lottery to get papers to come to the United States.

3: Years my dad spent here alone before he sent for me and my mom.

4: Years of useless English classes.

14: Friends I left behind. True, laugh-until-you-cry best friends.

52: Steps I climb to the tiny, airless box of an apartment we now live in.

57,600: Times I've wished I was back home.

231,100: Words I don't know in the English language. (According to the Oxford dictionary there are 231,100. We won't even mention the 47,100 obsolete words.)

I know I'm lucky. I know there are people who dream of coming to America. I know there are people who are dying to come to America. I know there are people who die to come to America.

But sometimes I don't feel lucky at all.

X+Y=MY ACTUAL NIGHTMARE

School smells different here. Back home, it was a sweet smell, something close to the sugared milk my mom made me when I was sick. Here it is like everything else: foreign. Like bleach and eraser.

By this third year of high school, I should be the girl who carries the flag in the processions, the one who gets away with just a little more than I could last year, with teachers who have known me since I lost my first baby teeth in my small school that went from kindergarten until the end of high school. All of that is erased now. But then there's this other feeling that ties have been unfastened, rules on stone tablets have been cracked. I have come to the land where everything is possible.

Math is the first class of the day. The classroom: too many posters, like a box lined with magazine ads. The kids: arm in arm and laughing even though the teacher is speaking. The teacher: fidgety and black-clad, impossible to understand.

Here's another thing: I'm overdressed. I'm in a stretchy black skirt, black tights, and a red bolero jacket. At home, I would practically be in uniform in this outfit. But here, the girls are in stretch pants and oversize sweatshirts, hair scraped up into scrunchies on their crowns, faces washed of makeup. One girl is actually wearing plaid pajama bottoms. I'm suddenly self-conscious of the extra time I took to elaborately curl and clip strands of my brown hair around itself so that it does more than just hang halfway down my back, not quite straight, not quite wavy, like it usually does. It would have been more fit for a party than for school even back home, but this morning it somehow felt like a good idea, like putting my best foot forward. Now I realize I look like the only kid who listened to her parents and dressed up for a party. Like I'm trying much too hard.

There's this, though: a cute boy is sitting to the left

of me. I'm relieved to have a normal thought, just: *this is a cute boy.* I let myself take a look at him sidelong. He's wearing a burgundy T-shirt with a line drawing of an old-timey diving helmet. His hair is combed, starting to kick up at the neck like it's been a week too long since his last haircut. He is everything I imagined American boys to be: Netflix-series handsome, with angular cheekbones and wide, beautiful lips, his skin perfect except for a smattering of spots near his temple, just enough of a shadow on his jaw to make it known he did not shave this morning, but does. He looks relaxed, bored, even, leaning back slightly, flicking a pencil around in long, knobby fingers. He looks like the world is exactly the way he expects it to be. I've noticed that about the Americans in my new town. So many of them look like they've lived lives empty of bad news, of unpleasant surprises.

"Ana?" the teacher says, flipping the longer side of her hair back, looking at a list.

I look around. Could there be more than one?

"#### ########## ## #####," she says. She waits, looking at me. She's expecting something.

My heart starts pounding. "#######," she tries again. To me, she could be saying anything. I took four years of English back home. I watched all kinds of subtitled American movies and television shows. It was one of the reasons I didn't worry about coming here: I knew this place before I got here. Or so I thought. Hearing English here, so fast, it's impossible to understand. She's just written a problem on the board. Does she want me to give her the answer? I squint up at the equation. I do know how to do it.

I walk to the front of the class, wind-tossed trees for legs. I can feel eyes on me, and hear a few snickers in the back of the room. I hear one girl say, "Check *this* out." She means me. I'm the "this." I should take some comfort that at least I understood that snickering.

I stand next to the teacher, waiting for her to hand me the marker. Her badly dyed hair covers half her face. She looks at me, confused. Giggles are popping up like popcorn in more parts of the class, and so I pick up an extra marker and quickly begin the problem. Two guys laugh louder in the back, and one slaps another on the chest backhanded. Still, the teacher says nothing.

I search my panicked brain for appropriate words, but all I can say is: "I do . . . math?"

The whole room bursts into laughter.

A ripple goes over the teacher's face, and confusion is replaced with pity. She feels sorry for me.

"Oh, honey, no," she says. "################## ######## #####." More words I don't understand. Finally, she picks up a book off her desk. She asks, slowly and greatly exaggerating her syllables, "You . . . have . . . book?"

Oh

Dear

God.

She asked me if I had the book, not to come up to the board and do a problem. I clench a fist and rub out what I've written on the board with the edge of it. More laughter. My insides turn to ooze and filter down to my knees. Please let me melt and slither away in a liquid version of myself. Preferably an invisible one.

She says something to the class that sounds scolding, but I can't make it out through the rushing sound in my ears, a sound like a river. I grab the book from her and make my way back to my desk.

Deep breath. Don't cry. Crying would make this so much worse. Still, the shame comes in waves and threatens to pull me down into full-on sobs.

Don'tcrydon'tcry.

The teacher talks, but I can't hear her, just the rushing in my ears. Then she sits down. Her desk seems too big for her. She's written a page number on the board, plus "1–7." People are scribbling. She must have assigned problems. I accidentally catch the eye of the boy next to me, the one with the burgundy diver's helmet T-shirt. He smiles at me.

I still want my desk to be sucked into another dimension with me in it, so I dart my eyes away.

I put my things in my bag. The book is huge and barely fits. I shove it in and close the zipper over it. I walk up to the desk. The tears are right under the surface. The teacher looks up again.

"Bathroom?" I ask.

Thankfully, that word is a sentence all its own.

I am

"I am" is the shortest sentence I know in the English
language.
"Soy" and "estoy" mezclados, like here there is only
one way to be, all permanent.
I am Ana.
I am from Argentina.
~~I have sixteen years.~~
I am sixteen years old.
I am in this place, a "soy" kind of am, not an "estoy"
kind of am.
In Spanish, "estoy" gives you a way out. Here "I am"
makes everything sound like an identity. Not a thing
that can pass, like in Spanish.
I am a poet.
I am a poet without words.
I am.
I am.
I am.

THE TROLL WHO LIVES
UNDER A BRIDGE

The next class is my ESL class, which means English as a second language. I walk toward it with relief. I can't wait to meet the other students who speak Spanish, talk to a teacher in Spanish.

Anything in Spanish.

The chairs are in one big circle, the desks pushed up against the walls. The class fills up quickly, and I'm surprised to be among such a diverse group of kids. Out in the halls, it's a sea of white faces, but here we are a range of different skin tones and identities. There's a boy wearing a turban, one Black girl with long braids that go down her back, two girls who look East Asian, and a boy with big brown eyes who could be from any number of places. Out there I feel the subtle scent of "foreign" on me, like all the other kids can somehow sense I'm from somewhere else. Something about my clothes, or how I do my hair, some nameless thing I can feel but not fix. Here everyone else has it too. And I imagine it's even harder for some of them than it is for me.

Then a thought occurs to me: *They all speak Spanish?*

Another white student walks up to the front of the room. He's in red high-top sneakers, jeans, and a T-shirt that says *The Clash* on it under an open button-down. His hair is cut surfer-style, and he taps a pencil, eraser down, as he watches everyone file in. Why is he up there? When the second bell rings, he clears his throat.

"I'm Mr. T.," he says. *Oh, he's the teacher.* "In case you were wondering, yes, *I'm* the teacher," he says very slowly. "Not *that* Mr. T. #### ####### ########?"

I look around. Everyone looks as confused as I do.

"We've got eight kids who speak almost as many languages here. #### ############# ##### ########## ###### with the big new ESL class, am I right?" He laughs. No one else laughs. It begins to dawn on me: If people who speak a bunch of different languages are in one class then that means . . . *ESL class is not in Spanish.* A class where not only do I not understand the teacher but to understand my classmates we also have to learn multiple languages.

Or we all have to learn just the one, which feels equally impossible right now.

He turns to face us. "Okay, ##### ############### ####, people. Who understands me?"

I tentatively raise my hand, because he's speaking slowly and I've caught enough of what he's saying from my television-show-and-lyrics and mostly-a-failure-English-classes-back-home English. Three other students do as well. The others look at us, a familiar panic in their faces, then raise their hands.

"Okay, that's good, that's good. This is my first year here. ########### ########## ####," he says with a smile. "#### our ESL book." He holds up a blue book with a bunch of cartoon people shaking hands. He points to a pile on his desk and asks us each to get one.

He has us turn to page five and then talks about something I don't understand. The disappointment that this class isn't in Spanish sits like a troll on my belly, the kind that lurks under a bridge and demands payment before you can cross. That's English—the troll that won't let me do anything until I pay him a price I can't cover.

The next thirty minutes pass by in a blur. As the clock winds down, the teacher starts going around the room, handing out notebooks from a stack. The one he gives me has a swirling pattern in red. I flip it open and the blank page stares back at me.

"These are journals. ##### ###### ##########. Write! Write in English. Things you see, ideas, poems, ####, recipes, whatever. Questions. Anything. Only English. Even if you only know one word, write that word. Look up the words you don't understand." He holds up his phone. "If you don't have a phone, ##### a dictionary. Like an app, but on paper." He laughs at his own joke. "I'll also be giving you some writing assignments to turn in."

The bell rings. That, at least, is one thing we all understand. The whole class gets up and starts filing out the door. I, for one, can't wait for this day, this never-ending first day, to be over.

"English journals! Write in them!" Mr. T. calls after us, but we are all already gone.

EATING CAKE AND HAVING IT TOO

Here's a thing that's the same: My mother still makes lentejas, which I hate, and chuletas, which I love. Her hemisphere has changed, but not her menu.

"Bernardo, no me digas que no vas a comer más," she chides my father. She always wants everyone to eat more.

"Gisela, English at home."

My mother frowns. It's ridiculous that he wants to tell my mother what language she can speak in the place where she lives. But I keep my face blank, because my father feels far away, like someone you spot way down the block and wonder if it's who you think it is. He annoys me in a way he didn't use to, like he's got just a bit more of a flinty edge to him. But the last time I lived with him, I had just turned thirteen. I'm different now too.

"Sorry," she says, rolling the *rr*'s hard, even though that's not how they say it here. "Is hard." My mom took English classes back home, after we knew we were coming here. Every Tuesday night she'd take the bus to an aunt's neighbor, who was Argentinian but went to college in Cleveland and who gave private lessons in exchange for sewing and stuff around the house. She was old, and smiled without moving her eyes. My mother didn't seem to like going there, but she did, without fail. Maybe that's why my father doesn't see how stifling it is to speak only in English at home. He thinks we learned enough back home. Or we should have.

"It's hard, yes, but is what better," he says. Easy for him to say, since he had a three-year head start. When we got picked for the visas, he came ahead and got a job as a driver and saved up while we settled things back home. We sold our little house and lived with my abuela and sent him the profit so he could buy his own car and make better money. So for three years he's been here, practicing. To him, English doesn't feel like being dunked in cold water. If it did once, he's forgotten.

The first month after he left us back home, the nights boomed empty. The neighbors turned up their collars at us as if bracing for a wind, pretending not to see us. "Ahí van las americanas," I once heard old Doña Dominga mutter when she thought I wasn't listening. *There go the Americans.* Or maybe she'd wanted us to hear.

That first month, my father WhatsApp'ed us every night. We were in different seasons but almost the same time zone. He was in a sweater and a scarf while I was in shorts. Later, when it came time for the brasero and gloves, he wore a flowered shirt he would never have been caught dead in back home.

"From a church," he said as he ran his hand down the front of it self-consciously.

We got into a routine. He said we'd start to only speak English to each other so that I could get ready for when we'd move to be with him. "Pero, Papi—" I began.

"English!" he'd say.

"I already takes English class."

"It's 'take,' so . . . more work to do. Ready for question one?"

That was his protocol. Three questions I had to

answer in English and couldn't answer with the same thing I'd said the day before.

"Ready."

"What did you learn in your third class today?"

My third class was a free period, but I didn't want to explain. I wanted to give him an answer that would make him happy. "I wrote a poem."

"What about?"

"That question two."

"No. It's a follow-up to one." He laughed.

"About water. Water so cold it feels warm in your bones."

"El Rio Mendoza," he said.

"Yes," I replied, trying to read the crinkles around his eyes. Was that sadness?

"Question two," he said. "What's an interesting thought you had today?"

I knew he liked this to be about current events, or history, or something that showed him I was awake in the world. "I wonder if France had king, he could . . . today."

"France doesn't have kings anymore."

"No," I said, the words fleeing me like skittish birds. "If today France had still the kings . . . the . . ."

"Monarchy?"

I had searched for that word in anticipation of our conversation but had forgotten it. "Monarchy, yes. If they still had monarchy, who would be king?"

"Have you found the answer yet?"

"No."

"I'll expect you to do it before tomorrow. Question three: What's a dream you have for when you come to America?"

I'd given him dozens of answers by then, every day a different one. I wanted to ride a taxi painted yellow, and eat a burger like the ones you see in the movies, which looked bigger and juicier than the ones you could get in el centro, and go to the top of the Empire State Building.

"I have a dream the words will come easy," I said.

I waited for the speech about how I should study more, practice and practice more, a speech I got about twice a week. But on that night, his shoulders shifted like he was bracing for a blow, and he muttered something about having to get up early the next day.

Eventually, the calls slowed to every couple of days, then once a week. At first, I was sad. But then, life swelled full. And then I wasn't.

By the time I saw him standing in the airport waiting area, I felt shy.

I knew this man, my father, and also I did not.

He knew me. And also he did not. I haven't shaken the feeling in the weeks since we got here.

My mother passes me more lentejas. She acts like she gets paid every time someone takes a spoonful of food. I shake my head.

"How is math class?" my father asks. I frown my annoyance. He adds, "A good job is important. You ask about engineering class?"

I blink at him. I want to unleash a torrent about everything I have to learn before I can ask what classes are available. But I don't know how. The frustration bubbles in me.

My mother, the ultimate reader of a room, cuts in. "I make cake," she says. She's made it, she means. She also means that if I don't eat more of these evil brown little beans there will be no cake. She *also* means that my father should back off a little. She's always meant more than she says, in any language.

I scrunch up my nose and take another mouthful.

"The Americans have a saying," my father says. "About cake. Eat your cake and have it too," he says.

"That make no sense," I say, annoyed at the lentils, annoyed to be speaking about English, annoyed to be speaking in English at all. "If you eat the cake, then you don't have anymore."

He shrugs, shoveling in another mouthful of lentejas. "Americans," he says, swallowing them fast. "They think anything is possible."

BREAKING ICE

My second day of school goes only marginally better than the first. I know how to find my locker, and I definitely know better than to go up to the board in math class under any circumstances. I kind of know how to get to my classes.

I slide into my seat in ESL class just as Mr. T. kicks off class by asking, "Okay, who thought yesterday's class was boring?"

There's a girl in a neat button-down sweater, so heartbreakingly neat. I wonder if I look as eager to be liked. Another girl, in jeans and a head scarf, stares at her desk. A boy with shaggy brown hair leans back in his chair.

This is clearly a trick question. My fellow ESLers are on to him too, because no one raises their hand.

"Okay. ###### ######## ####### ice breakers."

Ice breakers? I think I misunderstood. There is no ice anywhere in sight in this class. And I'm not sure why he'd want us to break it, anyway. I get this crazy picture of him bringing in a huge block of ice and letting us swing at it with sticks like it's a piñata until little shards of it are all over the floor. I would enjoy that, actually.

He must sense the general confusion, because he adds, "Ice breakers! Like . . . ######### ############ ######## exercises. Ways to get to know one another. This one is called #### and Lines." He holds up a sheet of paper. He's printed instructions off the internet. "Okay, so first, we're going to break out into groups based on the first letters of our names. A through G here!"

No one moves. We look at each other, searching for clues.

"You," he says, pointing at a boy with jet-black hair,

ice-blue eyes, and a compact, wiry build. He speaks even more slowly when he addresses us individually. "What's your name?"

"Neophytos," he says. I know how it's spelled because he's written it tentatively on the front of a notebook on his desk and I can spy it from where I sit. He's wearing a tucked-in button-down shirt and slacks. He's overdressed like I am. "Neo," he says more succinctly.

"Neo, okay, great. Not your turn yet. You?" he asks the boy next to him, the boy with the turban, beautiful brown eyes, and the coolest phone case I've ever seen, like an old-fashioned cassette player.

"Bhagatveer," he says.

"Okay, B name. B, right?" The boy nods. "Over here. Can you tell me again how to pronounce it?"

"Bhagatveer," the boy says quietly. The teacher smiles and repeats it.

"You?" He points at me.

"Ana," I say.

He looks visibly relieved that my name is short. "Ana. Here with the Bs." I walk over.

He goes through the rest of us until we're clustered in four groups.

"Okay, see? That's one thing we have in common.

Now, everyone who is wearing blue, come over here and stand by me."

He goes through several versions of this, colors we're wearing, whether we like to swim or bike ride better. Everyone falls into different groups each time. I guess the point is to show us we have something in common with everyone.

"Birthday season. Fall, winter, spring, summer." He points to different areas.

"In which country?" I ask.

He looks confused. "When is your birthday, Ana?"

"July," I tell him.

"Great, so summer. Over here."

I poke my index finger into my collarbone. "My country. July is winter."

Understanding shifts over his features. "Oh? Oh, yeah, I guess so, right. Southern hemisphere. Okay. Then winter." He points to a spot by the boy with the black hair and the cool blue eyes. Neo.

"Okay, everybody, ####### ##### ######## pretty even groups. Which is good because we're going to do this next exercise in pairs. Your job is to interview your partner and find out something interesting about them to share with the rest of us. Okay?"

I stare at the boy. We've been fated by our winter birthdays, and it feels slightly unfair since my birthday and his are in totally different winters. At least I think they are. The boy stares back at me. His eyes are quick, and he looks windswept, like the kind of guy who belongs outside. His skin is still warmly colored from the sun, and his face is framed strongly by sharp eyebrows that must give away his every mood. I don't even know what language he speaks, or if he speaks any English at all. Not that I speak so much.

"Hi," I say.

"Hi," he replies, accent thick.

I tell him where I'm from. "How about you?" I ask. He shrugs. I wonder if he understood the instructions.

I pull out my phone and I google a map of the world.

I point to him. "Your country?" I say, and hand him the phone.

"Qui-prei-o," he says, pointing to his chest. That does not help in the least. He tries to expand the map, but it doesn't zoom in as much as he wants it to. He points to the middle of the Mediterranean Sea. He furrows his eyebrows, confirming my hunch about how they give away his mood. He hands me back my phone, pulls out his, and googles on his own.

He shows me his screen. An island shaped a little like a lamb chop. Cyprus, it says.

"Speak Greek?" I ask. I studied that island in geography class back home. It's way on the eastern side of the Mediterranean, tiny, looking like it's about to be eaten by land from the north, east, and south. I know they speak Greek there. Turkish too, I think, at least on part of the island. In Spanish the name of it is Chipre, which sounds a lot like a chirping bird. I wish I knew how to tell him all this. Like: I see you. I know your country is small but I know about it.

He nods in response to my question. Yes to Greek.

I look around, and other groups are laughing, sketching things for each other on paper. By comparison, my partner looks like he's resisting interrogation.

I wait for him to ask me something. He doesn't. The silence stretches out awkwardly.

"Okay, I tell you about me," I try, recalling my English lessons from back home. "I like to write poetry. I love my family and . . . traveling." That's not quite what I want to say. Not all of it, anyway. I did love the airplane ride we took to get here, but "travel" makes it sound like something I've done. What I mean is that it's something I hope for. I want to see everything and everywhere.

There's more silence. He studies my face with robot precision. I wait for him to ask me something. He doesn't.

Finally, the teacher calls us back from our groups and goes around the room so we can all share what we learned.

"Neo likes cars," I lie, just to see if he'll react. He doesn't. Mr. T. nods. "That's great. Remind me to tell you about my first car. #### ## ### Mustang. I'll bring you pictures." Mr. T. points to Neo with his chin. "And what did you learn about your partner?"

Is that color on his cheeks? Or a smile breaking out on his face? "Ana like flies," says Neo.

The teacher laughs, along with a few of the kids who seem to get the ridiculousness of the statement. I turn to Neo. I wish for enough words to ask him what the hell he's thinking. He gives the beginning of a sheepish smile, the first one I've seen. He has a dimple, it turns out.

The teacher recovers. "Well, okay, we all like different things. Good." The teacher moves on to another group.

I lean over and whisper at Neo. "Flies?"

He puts his hands out by his shoulders, like wings. "Aeroplano," he says.

"Travel? Airplane? That's not 'flies.'"

"Sorry," he says, not looking at all sorry. "I forget word." His very blue eyes look like they are smiling at me.

The teacher finishes going around the room; I learn that Bhagatveer likes ice cream, and a girl named Adira likes video games. By the time he finishes, there are only ten minutes left. "Okay," Mr. T. says, clapping his hands. "Freewriting time. Take out your journals."

There's a collective groan as everyone pulls out their notebooks. I turn to a blank page.

In the last twenty-four hours, I've managed to fill up three pages: words I've overheard in the halls, the name of a song that was playing when my dad picked me up from school yesterday, even some words from the mail I brought in last night, which my mom threw away since none of it was addressed to our family. At first, I thought this notebook was going to be dumb, that I'd barely use it at all. But in a place where I'm too nervous to speak, it feels good to write.

To my left, I hear a scratching noise. I glance over and see Neo scribbling furiously in his notebook, and I can't help but wonder what he's writing. Is he doing the same thing as me, jotting down all the weird, inconsistent rules of this impenetrable language we now share? His eyebrows knit in complete concentration. I know the feeling behind that look, the experience of being completely engrossed in something.

When his body shifts, I see what he's doing. He's not writing at all. He's halfway through an exquisitely detailed drawing of a jumbo jet, its engines whirring, one small face waving from a tiny window. I can't tell whose face it is.

I guess you can be mysterious in any language.

Overheard in the hallway at school

Fuckface. A face that likes to do sex?
Doosh nozl?
Shit biscuit?
Duck butter?
Bananas. Like "crazy"? If I had to pick a fruit that is crazy, I'd pick pomegranates, with their juicy beads hiding in impossible recovecos, from which it takes an hour to free them.

If that's not bananas, I don't know what is.

EL OBJETIVO

I trail behind my mother. She's in a loose cardigan, her brown hair in a ponytail at the nape of her neck. In the short time we've been here, she's come to love this store, although I can't quite figure out why. At first, I thought it was called "Objective," like, "The objective of this story is to explain why my mother loves this giant store." Or at least that's what my translate app led me to believe. Then I saw the logo and understood the other definition—bull's-eye. How can a word mean both a purpose and something you aim at with a gun?

My mother wanders the store in a way she never did back home. She walks slowly and gazes at the

well-stocked shelves, the array of T-shirts with sparkles on them, the macramé pillows, the serving
platters, the yoga balls. It's not like we didn't have big
stores back home. Here we shop with a strict list and
a smaller budget, but it takes twice as long. Every few
aisles, she stops, picks up something new, and asks me
to translate the label. Like someone is going to ask her
to write a report on the contents of this store.

"What this say?" She holds a light-green container
out to me.

I study her face, searching for clues. What does she
want to know? She's hollow-eyed, her skin more mot-
tled somehow. Tired, maybe? And why is she enforcing
my father's English-only rule, when he's not even here,
when it's clearly so hard on her? She notices my hesi-
tation and gives me an arched-eyebrow look. Her best
compliance-compelling mom stare.

I sigh, scan the packaging, and punch the name into
my app. "Foaming soap for sonic faces," I say, reading
the translation from my phone.

She wrinkles up her nose. "What that mean?"

I shrug. She has a phone but insists on me translating everything for her, like I've developed some special
powers of understanding available only to teenagers.

We work our way through every aisle. The place

is massive. I imagine small clouds forming under its impossibly tall ceiling.

"Is this?" she says, handing me another package. A hair product.

I square off in front of her. "Ma," I say. "El Papi no está aquí. No tenemos que hablar inglés."

"English . . . ," she says to me.

"We don't have to speak English," I tell her. I think—

We don't have to do it this way.

We don't have to make it so hard.

We don't have to erase everything about us. At least not all at once.

—but I do not say it.

She sighs and studies her cracked cuticles. Her sweater hangs loosely around bony hips. Her hair is falling out of her ponytail. She never would have gone out to a store looking like this back home.

"Ana, tu padre piensa que esto es lo mejor," she says finally in Spanish. *Your father thinks this is best.* I notice she doesn't say she thinks it's best. She didn't use to hide behind his rules, especially not in the years it was just her and me.

She puts the bottle back on the shelf.

"We try," she says, her eyes earnest and wide,

something close to pleading. Or asking me to help and not hinder.

Tears of anger prickle the soft skin under my eyes. But when I look up, ready to tell her that this is not fair, that I want to go back to the apartment, that I can't do this anymore, I see her eyes are glassy with tears too. I notice that her face is lined in new ways.

Suddenly the meandering march through the store makes sense, clicking into focus like a camera that just needed a minute to take in the light. Maybe she is as lost as I am. Maybe the objective is to find our way, together. My heart feels tender for her. I've always known her to be a woman who knew how to do things, who to call, where to turn. But here, she doesn't.

Back home, when she was a girl, her family used to tell her she'd grow up to be a doctor, because she always would run to get a bandage when someone needed one, steady-handed, estomago fuerte. Because she always aced school. But they were poor, and she dropped out of high school to bring money in for the family. After leaving school, it was hard to go back, although she always meant to.

So much of her life has been unpleasant surprises. Even this, which she longed for and planned for, has left her adrift, far away from her sisters, from the place where she knew the names of everything. I can see it in the tight line of her mouth, in the hands she won't stop rubbing together. In the seeking of answers in the labels she can't read.

"We try," I tell her. "We try."

LA AMERICANA

Valentina calls me on WhatsApp. My heart sinks at the sight of her name on my phone. Not because I don't love her, but because of how much I do. She was born one day before me and we grew up basically like sisters. I was the bookish one, she was the science-loving one. She was my best friend, my confidante, my schoolmate. Now she's a face on a screen. Still, it's a familiar face, with her big, serious yellow-brown eyes and her smattering of freckles on her nose. I can tell she's braided her hair to make it wavy, the way she always would practice on me. I often tried to get out of it, since she pulled much too hard as she combed and braided. Now I wish she was close enough to do it.

I pick up.

"Ahí está la americana!" she says.

I smile. Seeing her, my old life rushes back in: walks in el centro, our mothers in a café while we roamed the stores on our own, feeling so grown up. Nights under el parral behind her house, picking fat grapes while her father scolded us from the kitchen window. Swapping clothes, and listening to music, and getting dressed together for our first formal dance.

I ask her how she is. She tells me that she's been chosen as the Reina de la Vendimia. It's a big deal, being reina. Vendimia is the grape harvest, and each neighborhood picks a reina for the parade. We used to talk about how great it would be if one of us could get it. She used to say it would be me. But now that everything has changed and it's her, I'm both happy and sad. Putting down a life to pick up another one is hard, a swirl of regret and excitement and what-could-have-beens and what-will-bes.

She asks me if everyone here is gorgeous and rich like in the movies. I snort-laugh. I remember what people used to imagine about being here. What I used to imagine. How do I explain that it's both everything we thought it would be, and also nothing at all?

As we're about to hang up, she holds up her jewelry box. I've seen it in her room a thousand times, quilted with delicate fabric on the outside, with a spinning ballerina inside that pops up when you open it. She pulls out the bottom drawer. It's got a roll of bills in it.

Valentina tells me that she's helping at the panadería on the corner after school. She says maybe soon she'll have enough to visit me.

I fight back tears. "Espero que sí," I say. I hope so.

BLUE BIRD

It feels like a different planet in this school sometimes. I have this image of me in a thick metal suit of *I don't understand*. Everyone else is used to this gravity, but it sucks me down into the chipped tile floor. There are wondrous things, too, though, on this strange planet: the smells coming from the cooking classrooms, and the teachers letting us listen to music in class with our headphones after we've done our work. There is a two-story atrium with delicate sculptures hanging from the skylights, papier-mâché birds suspended in midflight.

There is also math, where I can actually follow the

lessons. Math, where the cute boy sits to the left of me. Who knew math would be the bright spot in my day.

I glance at him out of the corner of my eye. He's in a forest-green T-shirt today with a sailboat stenciled on it in white, like a drawing you'd use to build the boat. On the shoulder closest to me, in script, it says *Sponge Diver Supply*. I copy the letters into my notebook. I'll look up each word later, like I do a hundred times a day. Sponge. Diver. Supply. I'll work out how they fit together. Or, like other times, I'll wonder what in the world they're doing in one sentence.

His hair isn't messy today. It's haircut fresh. What would it feel like to touch it? It looks soft, but with a bit of curl to it.

The teacher turns to the board and starts talking as if she's explaining the problem to the whiteboard itself. She's such a mumbler, there's no way anyone behind the second row can hear her. Luckily I've already covered everything she's explaining. Last year. Back home.

About five minutes into class, it's clear the teacher is only going to discuss the equation with the board. The boy opens the front flap of his textbook and pulls out a small stack of perfectly square pieces of papers of every color, each about the size of his palm. One has water lilies on it, bright pink on a watery background of green and blue. Another is a field of stars, metallic silver and gold on a field of deep blue. Another is a geometric pattern, reds and oranges, another a picture of a cupcake with yellow frosting. His hand lingers over them, then he slides one out. It's a repeating pattern of piano keys, the light ones a buttery ivory. He begins to fold the paper. I try not to stare too obviously, but the movement of his fingers captivates me. I just have to watch his nimble, elegant hands.

Whatever he's doing, he hasn't done it very much, because it goes slowly, as if he's trying to remember how. He bites his upper lip in concentration. It makes me notice his lips again, really a beautiful mouth. He looks like the gorgeous boys from the American movies Valentina and I would watch. *No, no, focus. Math.* But he makes a fold in the paper, runs a finger on it, then undoes it and tries to make the paper flat again.

I'm not very subtle because the boy looks me right in the eye before I can pretend I wasn't staring at him.

He smiles and whispers, "# #### #### math, but #### ### ## # bore." I catch "bore" because I remember it from a passage I read in English class back at home, about a child who escapes a boring day by finding a door in the base of a tree that leads to a land of fairies.

I smile back. "Boring. Yes," I say. My heart thumps at the thought that any minute I'm going to say something stupid. And, also: cute boy. Now that he's talking to me I've got an excuse to linger over his features, the planes of his face, the half smile.

He sticks his hand out into the aisle between us. "I'm Harrison, by the way. I ##### ### ## ######### ######."

I put my hand in his. It's warm. He squeezes. "Ana." Behind him, a blond girl cocks her head in our direction. Two other girls turn to look, one with straight bangs and penciled-in eyebrows, and another with inky-black hair. I've noticed them before. I've started to think of them as the Very American Girls in my head. I mean, obviously all the girls here are Very American. But somehow these look more so, like they would get picked for an ad, if the United States needed an ad. They look how we assumed back home that American girls would look, scrubbed faces and sharp eyes. Confident. Quick with a comeback. I focus on Harrison.

"Ana? Do you know anything about Algebra Two?" he asks.

I nod.

He launches into a long speech, complete with hand gestures and a funny voice. I give him my best "interested" look. But between how physically distracting I find him and the fact that I'm only catching like every fourth word, all I can do is hope it doesn't morph into "completely confused."

"Problems one through seventeen, page two hundred thirty-two," the teacher says from the front.

"Fuck," Harrison says. That word I know. I've made a game out of cataloging American curse words. We have lots of good curses at home, but some of the ones here are truly bizarre.

Everyone turns to page 232. Most kids open their notebooks and start writing, a few others stare off into space.

Harrison looks over at me. "## ### #### ##### ####?" He talks really fast. That's what's getting to me about English. I know some of the words, but everyone talks like they're in a race. Also, they don't move their mouths as much as we do in Spanish, so all the words sort of blur together. My mother says they always sound like they have a mouth full of potatoes.

He's asking me a question, but I have no idea about what. I smile and nod. Can't go wrong with that. I hope.

He opens up a binder he has under his notebook,

then clicks it open, takes out a piece of paper, and hands it to me.

Oh. He was offering me a piece of paper. I run his words back through my head. "Paper." I know that word. I should have caught it. "Thank you," I say.

He pulls out his own piece of paper. I turn to my textbook and start working on the problems. They're not too hard. It takes me less than ten minutes to finish them. I look up at Harrison. He's got two on his paper. He is staring at number three.

"Help?" I whisper helpfully.

He scrunches up his eyebrows. "I'm not gonna be much help," he says, shaking his head slowly.

No, no. "I help?" I say, and point first to myself, then him.

"Oh! You *get* this stuff? ## more ## # geometry guy. Yeah," he says, and pushes his page to the edge of his desk closest to mine. I squint to see what he's written. His handwriting is small and neat. He makes his sevens funny. His twos have an unnecessary loop in them.

I lean over. Harrison has gotten the formula wrong. I wish I could explain this with words, but I can't, so I just circle where he messed up. Then I write, in light pencil, how he should have set it up. I point back at the textbook, then lean over him to the section where the formula is explained. I make a circle over it there, keeping the pencil in the air so as not to mark the book, then back to his paper. I smile.

"Oh!" he says. "I see #### # ### #####!" He erases what he had on his paper, then writes it the right way. I point to the next step, and he does it, nodding, like something has clicked.

"Thank you," says Harrison. Then he says a bunch of other things. I wish I could understand more of what he's saying. Until this moment I hadn't realized how much I ache to just be *spoken* to—how are you? where are you going after school?—since I started walking around in a bubble of silence. Well, not silence really. A bubble of undecipherable noise.

He takes his squares of paper and holds them up in my direction, fanned out like playing cards. He runs his hand in front dramatically, like a magician enticing me to pick a card.

I scan them and point to a bright-blue one with different metallic shades, from turquoise to the dark blue of the ocean before nightfall. I love the smile that comes over his face when I do. He puts the rest away and starts folding that one. Fold, fold, turn over, fold. He hands me his blue creation. It's a bird, I think. The part that's supposed to be the beak skews slightly to the left, and one wing is bigger than the other, but it's the nicest thing that's happened to me since I walked into this school.

"Thank you." I smile, fighting the urge to hug the paper bird to my heart. *Get ahold of yourself, Ana.*

"No problem," he says. "Only nine hundred ninety-nine to go." Nine hundred and ninety-nine is a lot of paper birds. But then numbers were one of the first things they taught us in English class back home, so I'm pretty sure that's what he said.

The bell rings.

"Bye, Harrison," I say. He stands, gathers up his things. I stand too. He faces me, slinging his bag over his left shoulder.

He repeats, "Harrison," putting extra emphasis on rolling the *rr*'s. Trying to pronounce it like I did. He can't do it. That's another thing I've noticed about English: no double *rr*'s. "Say it again," he says.

"Harrison."

"First you teach me math, then you make my name beautiful."

I smile as I zip my bag. *Your name is beautiful,* I think, but is another thing I do not say.

I wish you could turn into an equation
So that I could understand everything about you.
I wish I could be like one of your paper birds
But sprout real wings
and fly free.

CAN I SPANK **YOUR** HOARDER?

Mr. T. collects our first assignments today. I'm a little embarrassed that the first piece of writing I've handed in is about a boy, but it's too late now. Besides, it's a poem, and I'm not sure I've translated everything correctly. He may not even understand what it's about.

Mr. T. has us write in our journals while he reads our work. At one point, his eyes flick up to me and then back down again. I wonder if he's reading my poem, and I blush. Perhaps he can guess what I was thinking about, after all.

A few minutes later, Mr. T. jumps out of his seat, almost as if sitting still for ten minutes has been as hard for him as it has been for us. He clears his throat at the front of the room and seems surprised when all eyes turn to him.

"And now for a change of pace." He opens his eyes wide, fingers playing with fingers in an almost childish show of thrill. "You guys all have your ######## ######### ######## in the office, right?" he asks. I, for one, cannot bear to dim his enthusiasm. I nod, although I have no earthly idea what he just asked. Around me, equally confused heads nod.

"Excellent. Excellent. I have a big car. Let's go." Mr. T. makes the "follow me" motion with his arm, then heads out to the hall. He leads us outside, to the parking lot, and to a beat-up gray minivan. He takes keys out of his pocket. The car makes that *tweep-tweep* greeting. His car? He's going to show us his *car*? Maybe to teach us the names of car parts or something? He did say something about a car to Neo during one of our first classes. It seems like the kind of thing he'd feel we needed to know. I haven't been here very long, but I've already learned that Americans think they can't fully live without their cars. At least the ones around here. There are more cars in the parking lot that belong to students than teachers, which is crazy to me.

He opens the back door. "In you go," he says. "A few of you in the third row so you can all fit."

Confused glances are exchanged.

"Come on! Short ######! ###### ############ #### ######## bell!"

Neo looks at me, then gets in. He hugs the far edge of the seat behind the driver. I go in after him, followed by the rest of my classmates.

Mr. T. closes the door, and it's silent. No one asks a question. It feels endless, but it only takes Mr. T. a few seconds to walk around the car to the driver's seat. He rumbles the engine to life and backs out of his parking spot.

He's . . . taking us away from school? *Can he do this?* Is this allowed? Or are we somehow witnessing him losing his mind and taking a bunch of students with him? He doesn't look like it, though. He looks like he's on vacation, smiling, chattering words I can't catch.

He takes a left at the light and pulls into a parking lot. The familiar yellow sign looms overhead. McDonald's.

He turns into the drive-through. "Okay, kids! ###### ######### more American than this! I don't want to teach you from a ### old book that gives you bullshit phrases like 'Excuse me, where is the library?' ##### ######## live here. So lunch is on me. Except you have to order."

The intercom crackles to life. "Welcome to Alana's. Can I spank your hoarder?"

I shrug my confusion at Neo. He half smiles. Mr. T. orders. Then the boy next to him does, surprisingly well. Mr. T. rolls down the window on Neo's side.

"I like fries," Neo says.

"Would you like fries with that?" crackles the faceless voice.

He looks at me. I shrug again. "Closer," I offer, signaling with my hand.

He leans out the window.

"Fries!" he says, louder.

"Got that," says the voice, annoyed.

"Burger," he says.

"Chicken tenders?" crackles the voice.

I suppress a giggle.

Neo turns to me, like he's not going to try and correct her. My turn. "Fries and Big Mac."

"Would you like fries with that?" she asks again. Mr. T. laughs.

I raise my volume. "Yes!" Mr. T. gives me a double thumbs-up.

"Anything else?"

The girls behind us go, then Mr. T. orders eight sodas, letting us off the hook on asking for those.

"Drive around," says the crackling voice.

We get to the window, and Mr. T. hands over a credit card and someone hands him two bags of food. He passes them back and drives away. In two turns, we're at the school.

He doesn't take us into the parking lot. He drives around the other side and stops in front of a giant tree with a bunch of picnic tables underneath it. I've seen this table at lunchtime before, its seats so full it looks like you would need a reservation. But it's not lunch period yet. Two lone kids are smoking near the back door. If Mr. T. sees them, he pretends he doesn't.

We make our way to the picnic table, and Neo sits next to me. He's got a bruise on his knuckle, but his all-telling eyebrows don't tell any tales today. A couple of the others take the spots across from us.

I pop a fry in my mouth. It's delicious. I haven't had much American fast food here yet, though back home I imagined that would be all I would eat. I take a sip from my drink. It is the size of a sand pail.

I look in my bag and realize Mr. T. has given me the chicken nuggets. Neo has a burger. I shake the container of nuggets at him. He smiles. He should do that

more. It changes his face in a way that's almost startling, all light and sunshine. He has a little dip in his
chin, and his teeth are perfect.

He lays his palm flat and makes a slicing motion
over it. The universal signal for half. He raises his eyebrows into a question. I nod. He opens the burger, cuts
it in half, and hands me one part. I open the nuggets.
I take one. Then he takes one. We fall into an easy
rhythm until they're all gone.

I take a deep breath and stretch my neck up to
the vivid blue sky. I love these unexpected gifts, these
moments you just can't plan for, a shiny penny in your
path. My abuela always used to say to me, "Barriga
llena, corazón contento." *Full belly, happy heart.* Maybe
Mr. T. knows that secret, too.

A NEW FRIEND

Art class is in a room that doesn't look like it started its life as a classroom. Pipes run up one wall, and every once in a while a clanging sound makes me jump. But it smells like paint and clay and has high ceilings and decent light. The far side opposite the wall of pipes is floor-to-ceiling windows. The walls that run between the two are covered in portraits on canvas going all the way up to an irregularly slanted ceiling almost two stories above our heads.

Everyone is in a uniform of black leggings and a loose top, or so it seems. Two guys have a game console under the table, and if the teacher hears the occasional ping or explosion from it like I do, she doesn't say anything. Another girl texts on her phone furiously, like she's having an all-out social media war of utmost importance. The teacher lets that slide, too.

The thing I like about art is that I can shut off my brain. No talking, not too much trying to understand. The teacher shows us something artsy at the front of the class, and we spend the whole period replicating it. We don't have art every day, and I look forward to it. We've made a print and an ink drawing. We've practiced shading by sketching fruits. Mine was a pomegranate, which was harder than I thought it would be. But it was an easy kind of hard, the kind with no consequences.

The teacher starts handing out sketch pads, and as people in the front rows begin turning toward each other, I realize she's breaking people up into pairs.

My neighbor turns to me. She is wearing a crop top and leggings with studded ankle boots. "You and me," she says. My eyes flick over her face to read if she's disappointed or not. I can't tell.

"Speak Spanish?" she says.

I let out a big breath. No one has asked me that here yet.

"Sí. ¿Cómo supiste?" I ask.

"You're one of the ESL kids," she says simply, in English, but I catch all the words. She jerks her head at the teacher. "Esta dice que hablemos."

I take a careful look at her. Metallic blue eyeshadow arcs around her yellow-brown eyes. Her contouring is runway ready, but perhaps a bit much for ten a.m. in a high school. Still, she looks like she's preparing for the former and not caring so much for the latter.

"¿Cómo te llamas?" she asks. Her accent is different, not from my country, but her Spanish is good. Relief.

"Ana," I say.

"Altagracia." She introduces herself with a toss of her curls, which seem to live independent of her.

I smile. "Nice to meet you," I say in English.

"Tú primero." She signals to my pad, indicating I should sketch her first.

I look her up and down, wondering how I'm going to sketch someone who seems like she's got the volume turned up on life. How to capture everything she's got going on?

She reads my face. "Okay. I'll go first," she says.

She narrows her eyes again, studies me through her eyelashes. They're so long I thought they were fake at first, but they look so real, they might just be. She says,

"You have good skin. You should let me do a video on you. I have ten thousand followers on Instagram, you know. I do makeup."

I smile. "Gracias." I take the compliment though I can't imagine ten thousand people seeing my face. Everything about her screams "look at me," whereas I spend most of my time wishing I could walk around in a helmet. What would it be like, not to hide? I didn't use to feel this way, I realize. Hiding is new. Hiding is not *me*.

"It is nice people . . . see you . . ." I tell her. That's not quite what I mean. "I want people to . . . see . . . me . . . too." Ugh, I'm such a nerd. *Why did I say that?*

The sun comes out from behind a cloud and makes her eyes look almost see-through. She doesn't blink. Her brash attitude leaves her for the moment, and she's not her carapace of fierce nails and geometric side-shave. She's just a girl with round eyes and a steady gaze full of curiosity and another thing. What is it? Not pity but a distant relative, something closer to protectiveness.

"I can help with that," she says in English, and for once I understand every word.

ONE THOUSAND PAPER TOW TRUCKS

Over the last few weeks, Altagracia has kept her word, and we've hung out a few times. She took me to Green Man, a café in town where I got the most enormous sundae I've ever seen. Sitting with her feels a little like having a spotlight turned on, and suddenly I remember what it's like to have everyone say hello when they go by. It's just Altagracia's reflected light, since she's the one they all know, but it feels good. I'll take being a moon over being a black hole any day.

My English is getting better, little by little; Mr. T. gave me an A on my poem. He didn't write any comments on it, so I'm not sure what he liked about it.

Since then, he's had us turn in a few more assignments. The more I write in English, the more comfortable I get. Sometimes, if I let myself feel words instead of focusing on them hard, I see inside their shell into something familiar. *Precious and precioso. Arbol and arboreal.* Others are entirely foreign but hold a little pearl of surprise in them, like the word "beautiful." How better to say that than "full of beauty"? English holds gifts and challenges. I think about it all the time, like a constantly unraveling mystery. It's hard to turn it off at night, when it's time to sleep. There is still so much to learn. But there are so many words that are mysteries to me, keeping me from saying everything I want to say.

And then there's math class, where, luckily, I can gaze at Harrison.

I check him out from the corner of my eye. Messy hair in the back, like he left his house in a hurry. Stubble on his jaw. A blue button-down shirt and black jeans that make his legs look long. He's distracting, every day in a new way.

Harrison pulls out his box of papers, opens it, and picks one colored paper square. Yesterday it was a bright-yellow flower. The day before it was blue penguins. It baffles me, because all semblance of what's printed on the paper goes away when he folds it into the bird shape. But maybe that's the appeal. Only he knows what's inside, the secret pattern.

Well, him and me, although I try hard not to seem like I'm looking.

He makes about three paper birds per class. He's gotten more efficient, his nimble fingers handling the paper with more certainty. But even though he's done in a few minutes, he stops at three instead of continuing to make them the whole class. Then he puts the blank papers at the bottom of the box, and the newly folded birds to one side. The box is getting more crowded since the first day he started.

I keep the one he gave me in the front pocket of my backpack, in a smaller section behind the slots meant for pens. It's just big enough for the paper bird, and I make sure not to put anything else there so it won't get wrinkled or torn. I'm sure he's forgotten that he made it for me, but it makes me happy that it's there, the first tangible sign of friendship I got here.

The teacher turns away from the board just long enough to say, "Study time!" We are having a test tomorrow. She steadfastly avoids talking to us if she can help it. I reach into my backpack for a pencil to work the practice problems.

Harrison leans over and whispers, "You still have the origami I made you."

I look down at my bag. I thought it was tucked in, but it was visible when I reached for the pencil. *Mortifying.* I learned that word the second week I was here, when I saw it in a passage in class and looked it up. It's a perfect word, so close to the Spanish word for death, *muerte.* Because isn't embarrassment a little like dying inside?

I smile weakly at him.

"I'm making them for my sister," he says. I turn to face him. His eyes make their way around my face, to my neck. Heat creeps up there.

"Your sister? How old?" I ask. I sound like a child who doesn't know the connecting words, a rusty faucet making noise as it struggles to run clean.

"Oh, way older. I was the oops baby. She's twenty-six."

I laugh. I've never heard it put that way, but I understand it instantly. *Oops baby.* Yes. My mother was la sorpresita. The little surprise.

"She's getting married. Her fiancé is from Japan," he adds. I glance up at the front of the room to see if the teacher is watching. I catch a flash of straight black hair turning away. The girl who watched us the other day. She whispers something to the girl with the straight bangs, one of the Very American Girls. The teacher is busy pretending the whole class isn't chatting.

"Japan?"

"She went to study abroad there one year, fell in love. She's getting married in a few months. That's why the ########."

"The . . ." He used a word I didn't understand.

He pulls out his notebook, writes it with his steady handwriting, turns it around for me to see. C-R-A-N-E-S. He pantomimes folding paper.

Oh. The folded things he's making. Cranes must be another word for folded paper creatures.

"You will bring . . . cranes? To sister?"

"Yes. I was googling how . . . I just wanted to do something ################# ######## for a present. So . . ." He shrugs. "Cranes."

I hold up a finger and check "crane" on my translate app. Maybe that will be my word for today.

It translates to grúa, which means tow truck. That cannot be right. I scrunch up my nose.

"What?" he asks. I google a picture of a tow truck for him. "This is crane?" I smile.

He laughs. "Man, that app does not always seem

helpful, huh? It led me astray constantly when I took Spanish in middle school. Here, hold on, let me."

He takes my phone with easy familiarity. Then he turns it back around to me. A long-necked white bird with black tips on its wings flies against a bright-blue sky.

Oh. *Crane is a kind of bird.* I laugh. How can a tow truck and a bird share a name? I'll add this to my list.

"They are supposed to be good luck," he says. "It is said that if you make someone one thousand paper cranes, you will have good luck. And they will too."

"I see."

"I've figured out that if I make three per day, I'll be done a week before the wedding. This teacher is totally out to lunch."

I nod. This teacher never eats her lunch in class, so I don't know what he means there. But, okay.

"I like ####### ########### #######. Kind of slows me down."

There's so much I wish I could ask him about—does he have other brothers and sisters? What's his favorite subject? How did he come to like that band whose sticker is on his box of cranes?—but I can't catch any of the words needed to form those questions. They swim in my brain, some visible, some shapeless, but none want to coalesce into sentences. It's so frustrating. It's like someone stole all my words.

The bell rings. Math is last period today, so it's time to leave. He says, "I go out the Smith door. Which way do you go out?" A tingle runs up my body. The thought of walking anywhere with him makes my skin feel alive. I bite the edge of my top lip.

"Smith door," I lie. I didn't even know the doors had names. But whatever door he's heading for, I'm headed there, too.

He gets up, gets his bag ready faster than he normally does. I sling mine over my shoulder. "C'mon," he says. He walks down his row, and I mine. At the front of the rows, he takes a step in my direction, and I feel the warmth of his body, smell the scent of his clean clothes. We stand next to each other while kids stream out of class around us. He starts to walk, and I do too. We bump into each other.

"Oh, I'm sorry," he says with a laugh. He holds out his arm. "Ladies first." For a second, I want to grab his hand and hold it. Or pull him toward me, and we will have our first kiss here in our math classroom. Which is an impossible idea, of course. I can't do that.

But maybe one day the impossible will be possible.

Same but different

Someone mentioned the right to bare arms
It took me weeks to figure out it was bear, not bare
A girl was talking about high waste pants in the hall
And I didn't know what that meant either
And when I finally figured it out it all came rushing
over me, the foolishness of my confusion.
Everything is a riddle.

Content: the stuff that fills my ESL notebook. The
things I write.
Content: how I want to feel here.

Close: what my father wants me to do. Close the door
on everything that came before
Close: how I want to feel. To someone.

I want a piece of peace

A week without feeling weak

A scene I've seen before.
I want to be whole, complete, unabridged, intact.

WHEN THE GOING GETS TOUGH

Classes are not at the same time each day. They cycle in some pattern I haven't fully figured out yet, something about A days and B days, all the way through D days. Today is a C day, and that makes ESL the last period of the day. I'm relieved to almost be going home. The hall is thick with bodies and people free a period early.

Neo is almost at the door to our ESL classroom. I want to say hi to him, but I remind myself we're not really friends, just classmates. Neo isn't watching where he's going, and it happens almost in slow motion: A boy with army-short hair is standing with his back to Neo, closing his locker door. His jeans have bright-red stitching, and his black T-shirt is skintight, an even-sided cross glowing in gold on it. I don't know him, so I can't explain the tingling of alarm, except that I know his type. He looks like the kind of boy who believes the world is the way it is for his benefit.

The boy turns and crashes straight into Neo. He glares at Neo. For a sickeningly slow moment, he stands back and ugly things play over his face: disgust, maybe. Anger. I quicken my step because I've seen that look, and about half the time it ends up in someone taking a swing. The air between them crackles with something bigger than a simple accidental bump.

"Watch where you're fucking going," the crew cut boy says. Neo holds his eyes steady, not escalating anything but not stepping away. Finally he turns around and goes into the classroom.

Inside, Neo throws himself into his chair like he's mad at it. I slide into mine. I can feel the anger radiating off him.

Mr. T. makes his way to the front of the classroom. On the board, he's written several lines:

A bird in hand is worth two in the bush
A stitch in time saves nine
Have your cake and eat it too

Put lipstick on a pig
Don't be a wet blanket

"Hello, everyone, settle in. Today we're going off book. The more I read your assignments, the more I realize one of the hardest things about learning English is understanding the phrases that really just don't make sense ###### ###### an app. Every language has them, ######### ########### in groups of two. We'll keep these groups ###### semester, so you can get used to working together. I'll hand ######## paper with ########. First I want you to talk to each other and ######## means. Then you can use your phones ####### in the back to look up the meaning. ########? Hopefully we'll have a few laughs."

He pairs us up, and I get Neo. I can almost see the angry little cloud of squiggles over his head, still vibrating from the encounter in the hallway. Mr. T. hands us our slip. It reads: *When the going gets tough, the tough get going.*

It's got one of the dreaded "ough" words in it. I have made a list and none of these rhyme. *Cough, tough, bough, although.* It is baffling.

I look at Neo. "You want to try to figure this out?"

He shakes his head. His expressive eyebrows telegraphing universal frustration, his head clearly still out in the hall.

I stare at it. We're supposed to guess what it means first, before looking it up. I look at the first part. *When the going gets tough.* When the road is rocky? When it is difficult to leave? When it's hard to say goodbye?

Getting nowhere, I look it up on my phone. *When things get hard, people who are tough try harder.*

I breathe it in.

I don't know if I'm "the tough," but I do know I want to be. I know that being here and learning English is tough. I know that it must be tough for Neo.

"Hey, Neo?"

He looks at me.

I slide over the slip of paper Mr. T. gave us, then I show him the meaning on my phone.

He looks at the words a long time. Then a slow smile spreads across his face. Not the kind that lights up his face, but a quieter type. He takes my phone and starts typing. For a second, I wonder what he's doing when I realize he's in the translate app. He's writing me a note, translating what he wants to say from Greek to English.

When he finishes typing, he shows me the screen.

I would like to argue back to that guy. Although punching is part of the universal language.

I laugh and take the phone back. *Have you ever been in a fight?* I translate from Spanish to Greek.

Neo's eyes widen, surprised by my personal question. He shakes his head.

I figure I've already started down this road, so I'll just keep going. We don't know each other well, but I sense that he may be as tired of walking around apart from everyone as I am. So I ask another question via the phone. *Do you miss home?*

He types it in. *Yes. I miss dancing.*

I cannot picture him dancing. "What kind of dancing?" I ask out loud now.

Nightclubs. No nightclubs here, he types, adding the sad emoji.

It's like that back home, too. I've been surprised by how little the kids here have to do at night. Back home, we were out every Friday and Saturday night, and there were clubs that were just for teenagers.

"How long you live here?" I ask. We have practiced some basic questions in class, and I try one out.

"Four month," he answers.

"Why?" I ask.

"Father," he tells me. It's not a complete explanation, but I sort of know what he means.

"Your whole family come?" I ask. Our questions may be only a few words, but we are talking. In English.

He shakes his head, turns back to the phone, and types out a message. *Mother and sisters all stayed home. I came with father because his job bring him. He tell me to come because my parents thought it would be good for me to practice English so I could succeed in college.*

"Will you go back soon?" I ask. It surprises me that the thought of him going back makes me a little sad.

He shakes his head. *I want to be an architect. The architecture school I want to attend is here*, he taps out carefully.

"What do you want to build?" I ask.

He takes the phone and shields it from my view as he types his answer. Then he shows it to me, beaming a big smile, the full one, chin dimple pronounced. *EVERYTHING*, it says. He lights up like I've never seen before.

We talk more, with and without the phone. He tells me about the building that first made him think about becoming an architect, on a vacation to Athens. I tell him about a story I once read, about a boy who builds a building so big at the end he doesn't know how to get out of it. Before I know it, I look up at the clock and realize that class is almost over. Mr. T. starts going around the classroom and handing back our assignments, speaking to us in turn about them. For a moment, I'm nervous—I've gotten more adventurous with my assignments lately, have started taking more risks in English. But that also means more opportunities to mess up. I know I make mistakes, as hard as I try not to. If he's grading for grammar and spelling, I am probably toast.

He stops at Neo's. "This piece you wrote made me think of this article," says Mr. T. I glance at the computer printout that Mr. T. puts on Neo's desk: *The Glossary of Happiness*, it says. I make a note to ask Neo about it later.

When Mr. T. sets my latest poem down on my desk, I realize there was nothing to be worried about. I got another A.

"You're a poet, Ana," Mr. T. says. "You're a poet in English, too. Keep writing. Okay?"

I smile. It feels like someone cracked a door in a dark room and suddenly I can begin to see shapes around me.

Ever since I arrived, I've been fumbling around in

the dark with English, trying to find a place where I belong. I still don't know, but I have a glimmer of an idea now, the tiniest light.

Mr. T. stands expectantly over my desk, waiting for my response. Luckily, my answer is the first word I ever learned in English. "Yes," I say, smiling. "Yes."

The ough in ouch

It's tough when you cough
When you have no dough (or moola or Benjamins—
who are the Benjamins, anyway, and why is it all
about them?)
And you think that lough should be spelled lough,
but it's low
But it's bow
As in you bow your head
Because it hurts that the language in this new
country seems to be trying to make you mute
When you have so much to say.
It makes my heart sore.
But it makes me want to try hard.
And soar, up, up, up to the sky.

RUNNING A RELAY

Forks on plates. Scrape. Click. Scrape. I remember reading somewhere that you're not supposed to let your fork make noise on your plate when you eat. Or maybe that's with soup. It's exactly the kind of politeness rule my mother would bug me about, once upon a time. But family dinners have gotten pretty quiet under the English-only blanket. If you can't think of the word in English—and most of the time I can't, and neither can my mom—silence is a safe alternative. If my dad notices how silent he's made dinners, he doesn't let on.

"How is school?" he asks, finally.

"Okay," I respond.

"What's favorite class?" I'm pretty sure he missed a word there, but I don't feel sure enough to correct him, even though there would be a sweet sort of satisfaction in it.

"Math is good," I say.

He is pleased by this. "Yes, math is good." We sound like a show for first graders. There's more under the surface, of course. Math is good because a job that takes math—engineering, medical school—is the kind of job my dad has told me more than once I should strive to get. I don't hate the idea, since math comes easily to me. But I also don't love it, either. I don't like the shove in any direction. There's so much for me to take in, and I kind of want to stand in this moment before being pointed at the next.

As soon as I think this, I feel guilty. My family is not running a marathon. We're running a relay. My parents have gotten me this far. Everything I do is to get us further. I carry their hopes along with my own.

My mother's phone rings. The tone hasn't finished its first buzz when she's scraping her chair back. She makes her way wordlessly to their bedroom. It's one of my aunts, probably, or maybe my abuela. There used to be a rule against taking phone calls during dinner, didn't there? I reach back to another time, another place, another table.

I can't remember.

I call Valentina. It goes to messages. I don't leave one.

THE CLUB FOR BREAKFAST

Walking into ESL later in the week, I spot Harrison in the hall. He leans back on a locker, talking to the Very American Girls from math. Harrison looks at me and waves, and they follow his wave like heat-seeking missiles. I try to wave and also casually pretend I'm not waving, which is as awkward as it sounds.

Neo slides into his desk right before the bell. Mr. T. walks in a full minute after the bell, surfer hair shaggy, button-down shirt crumpled over corduroy jeans, fabric worn at the knees. Teachers never dressed like this in Argentina. It slightly thrills me, like the rules are suspended here.

Today we slog through a lesson on verb tenses, run and ran, not runned, which would be more logical, that kind of thing. It makes me wish I runned away, but I sit still.

Finally Mr. T. puts the book down, takes a breath, and says, "This stuff really can be boring, right? I don't know how you do it."

I sidelong a glance at Adira, who meets my eyes from across the way. She arches her eyebrows at me. Neo sits up straighter.

Mr. T. walks up to the board and speaks as he writes a list of words. "Okay," he says. "We'll go around the room. Are you a princess, a brain, a jock, a rebel, or a recluse?"

I google "recluse" and go to images. It is a type of spider. A pretty hideous one.

He turns to us. The room is filled with the silence of confusion.

"Oh, come on now. Don't make me feel old. #### ## ### # you must have seen *The Breakfast Club*, no? It's a classic."

Bhagatveer nods shyly. Everyone else still looks confused.

Mr. T. approaches us, turns a chair around, straddles it. "*The Breakfast Club*, people. A holy ###. A guide for living. A ### #### ## of everything that means something in life. Love. Self-worth. Togetherness."

More blinks.

"It's a movie." He sighs.

Oh.

He gets back up. "Look, here's the deal. I'll cover this book stuff because . . . well, it will help you. ### #### ## ###. If there's anything more American than *The Breakfast Club*, ##### #### ######. So that's your homework. Go watch *The Breakfast Club*."

I glance at Neo. He gives me a perplexed little shrug.

"And, ##### #### ### #### #### ## #### school library has two copies, plus we've got streaming subscriptions too. Not that I had anything to do with that." He smiles mischievously. "You can watch it in one of the viewing rooms. We'll discuss it next time."

The bell rings and I try to picture going to the library. Asking for the movie. Hoping someone else hasn't gotten it first. Watching a whole movie, no doubt confused most of the time. But I don't want to disappoint Mr. T. either.

Neo's face betrays similar worries. He turns to me. "Movie . . . we watch?"

I nod. Obviously. It's homework. I always do my homework.

He points to his chest, then to me, then back. *"We* watch?"

Oh. *He means together.* I like that thought better, someone to help me figure out this whole new system. And maybe understand the movie too.

"Yes." I nod.

There is an expression I have learned in America: misery loves company. I think it means that if you are unhappy, it is good to be with someone else unhappy, too. But for the moment, I actually do not feel unhappy at all. I guess happiness loves company too.

I smile at Neo. "See you in the library."

BUCKLE UP, HONEYS

Here are two things I didn't expect. Altagracia's car smells like a meadow full of flowers. And she drives like my grandmother, if my grandmother could drive. *Someone's* grandmother. You'd figure that someone whose appearance seems to scream "I don't care what you think" would care a lot less about speed limits and traffic laws. But she comes to a full stop at every stop sign for a beat too long, and signals meticulously. Romeo Santos plays in the background, but it's almost too faint to hear.

We're on our way to her house to do a makeup tutorial for her Instagram. I'm weirdly nervous. I'm on her curl side, not her shaved side, and as she talks they sway to their own rhythm.

"You know, I wouldn't have guessed you're from Argentina when I first saw you," she says, then rolls her eyes. "That will probably work in your favor here, sadly."

I think about that for a moment, what my lighter complexion seems to signify here. How my family goes unnoticed until we open our mouths. But back in Argentina a white girl who speaks Spanish isn't all that surprising, since we are a nation of immigrants who speak Spanish.

"Anyway, I know it's hard to be new here," she says. "The people #### #### know #### #### 'different.'"

"How long have you lived here?"

"My parents met in New York at one of my mom's art shows, but when their careers took off, they moved here to, you know, be all suburban and shit. It was a big deal, and they thought ###### ### #### favor, bringing me to a place like this." She gestures again. "You know, the kind of place where I have to drive extra carefully so I don't get stopped. I was five. It was . . . it was a favor like ###### brussels sprouts are a favor?"

I'm not sure I got all that right. But she goes on. "So I grew up with all these blanquitos, but after my parents split, my mom moved back to the DR, and I spent at least part of every summer there. So ###### ###### ####, bouncing from the city to suburbia to Santo Domingo, with people I was told were my people, and who were, but not too, you know?"

I nod. I'm not sure I know. But I'm beginning to understand, maybe just a little, what it's like to be from more than one place. And thus from no place at all. Altagracia seems like she's so from here, with all the people she knows at school, but she's also had to deal with feeling different.

She turns onto a wide, treelined street. It ends in a giant circle with a small, perfectly manicured island in the middle. Red bushes, lime-green bushes, perfectly round mounds of white flowers, and a tree that looks like it just got a haircut. Every house around the giant circle looks big enough for several families, like a house you'd see in the movies. Is this where Altagracia lives?

Altagracia pulls into a driveway to the right—also a circle—and drives around to the front of the house. Every bush in the front of the house looks as severely angular as the ones on the little island in the middle of this dead-end street, box shapes and perfect spheres, like someone is allergic to letting plants grow how they want to.

We walk up to the door and she punches some numbers into a keypad. No key. Inside, the ceiling soars like a church. Everything is beige with white trim. The walls. The curtains. Straight ahead there's a glass table with a big glass sculpture. It glints as the light hits it.

"Welcome to our humble abode. My dad is afraid of color. #### ######### ##### the neighbors will think we're too ethnic. Come ### #### family room." I am listening but also trying to take in her house. I have never been in a house this big.

She walks me into a sunken room. More beige on the wall, white on the couches. She leaves and comes back with a pitcher of lemonade and two glasses. How do people who have houses like this also go to school with people like me who just got here and have nothing?

"Where is everyone?" I ask as she sits next to me.

"My dad works crazy hours. You'd be surprised just how many dental emergencies #### ####### #####. #### ###### many people want to have ##### teeth the size of #######. His girlfriend . . . who knows. This one's kind of new, so I never know if ##### pop in or not."

"Your family must be proud of your dad."

"They are," Altagracia says. "But he also frustrates my Abuelita." She laughs. "The family might have been happier if he'd just married a nice girl and stayed with her, you know? Although they do love saying there's a dentist in the family. We're the definition of making it to them."

I take a moment to wonder what it will mean for us to make it. It's more than I know how to talk about. "So you do makeup?" I ask, changing the subject. The words feel awkward on my tongue. *Do* makeup?

She lights up. "Well, ##### ####### ####### watching YouTube. Muchas de las blanquitas #### #### not what I needed. Kind of like when I first moved out here and no salon knew what to do with my hair. So I figured out how to do it myself. I knew I couldn't be the only one. I just decided . . . what if I try? I did a video on my phone and posted it on my Finsta. And, like, #### ####### followed me on there said nice things, ##### ###### ##### I didn't know liked it too. And then I read up on people #### ###### making money, and I thought, 'I'm smart enough to do that.' Build a following. Create a skin line, maybe. All natural, #### ##### ## help people? So here I am. You'll be my first 'guest model.'"

"Oh, wow." I am jealous of her focus when I am just aiming for survival. I want some of what she has, that limitless confidence.

"Anyway, tell me about you. Are you liking it here?"

Am I liking it here. I don't know the answer to that. There's nowhere else now, I know. But the thought of always feeling like a fish out of water is too big to hold sometimes.

"Is okay," is all I say.

She narrows her eyes at me skeptically.

"You like boys? Girls? Both? I like girls myself."

I smile at the question. It feels pretty American that she didn't assume but asked. "Boys." It's none of my business, but the question falls out of my mouth before I think about it. "Is it okay with your parents?" I had a friend in Argentina who had a hard time coming out because as much as things have changed, some people can still be intolerant.

"Surprisingly, yes. I know it's not always like that. But luckily my parents were pretty cool. My mom's an artist, and they have all different kinds of friends. It was touch and go there for a while with some of my more judgy aunts. We're good now, though.

"Anyway, back to you. Anyone at school in particular?"

I feel heat on my neck. "I don't know."

She jumps up, lands back down on the sofa in perfect cross-legged position. "Oh my God, you *do* know! Your face just gives it all away. Who is it? Spill!"

I look away, smile despite myself, smooth the front of my pants. "There's a boy in math class. He's just nice. There's nothing."

"Who?"

I want to start the friendship with honesty. But is this embarrassing? Do girls like Altagracia have crushes on people they barely know? I have seen everyone in the hallway saying "What's up, Gracie" and giving her high fives as she walks past. She is obviously someone people like. It makes me shy to admit the nerdier parts of myself, the parts that swoon over a guy who has barely only told me his name.

"Harrison."

"Harrison?" she asks.

I nod.

"*Harrison?*" she asks again, like she heard wrong. She sounds so confused that a thousand scenarios start to play out in my head. Maybe he's got a girlfriend. Maybe he doesn't like girls? Maybe he's already told her he doesn't like me? Okay, no, that last one is paranoid.

She laughs. "C'mere," she says. She stands, and I follow her up a beige-carpeted staircase to an enormous landing with ceilings twice as tall as I am. As soon as she opens the door, I can tell it's her room. It's the opposite of the beige house. Vibrant walls a color between pink and orange. A huge makeup mirror like the old-fashioned movie stars used to have, with big round light bulbs all around it and a thousand magazine cutouts of made-up faces. And opposite all this, a bed bigger than my parents' bed.

She leads me to the window. The house next door is far, but we can see straight into one of its windows on the second floor. The walls are navy blue and there's a band poster I can't quite make out. There is a string of perfectly manicured evergreens between this house and that one, but they're no taller than the first floor.

She points theatrically, a game show host displaying the brand-new car you've just won. "That's Harrison's bedroom," she says.

I turn to her. "What?"

"Harrison is my neighbor. He's been my neighbor for, like, ever. We once tried to run a string from his room to mine so we could #### ####### ####

messages. Marbles, one time. It was this ####
thing. We were like eight. The string kept
breaking. Our parents were pissed."

"He's your neighbor?" I ask, still catching up.

Suddenly, as if to prove her point, Harrison walks
past the window. She screeches, which makes me
screech. She pulls me down to the carpet.

As we crouch there she says, "So Harrison, huh?"

I nod.

She shrugs. "All right. I wouldn't have guessed
bland white boy is your type, but at least he's a nice
one. Aunque un poquito soso, ¿no?"

Bland? She thinks Harrison is bland? "¡No es soso!"

"Relax." She laughs and leads me back downstairs.
"So-so is in the eye of the beholder. Speaking of which,
time for your makeover."

I smile that soso and so-so are the same in English
and Spanish, although I don't think they mean exactly
the same thing. But somehow the two languages
started in different places and made their way together
in "soso."

We go to a room off the family room where Altagracia has what looks like a whole film studio set
up. Umbrellas with the lights inside. A fancy-looking

camera on a tripod. A low table covered with makeup, and another makeup caddy with enough tubes, palettes, and brushes to stock half the department store makeup section.

She waves her arm. "Voila. ##### ######. Where the magic happens."

She walks over to the camera, makes an adjustment, then flips on the lights. I squint. They're really strong. Altagracia turns to the camera and puts on a full-wattage smile.

"Hi, gorgeous! It's me, Gracie. I'm here with my beautiful new model, Ana. Doesn't she have just perfectly smooth skin? This is without primer, people. It's insane. Today we're going to give Ana a kissable ###### like you would not believe."

I smile, not sure what else to do.

"You'll remember I did a recent video on how to tone down your lips to a soft nude for things like a job interview? You can find a link to that video in the comments below. But buckle up, honeys, because this tutorial is not that."

Altagracia mutters to herself, rummaging through a bag. "I'm not sure I've got foundation light enough for you. This will have to do." She puts the foundation on my lips. It feels like wet chalk.

"Okay, first we start with a neutral base." She whispers to me, "You repeat it."

Me, through wet chalk: "Okay, honeys, we begin by putting on a neutral base."

She laughs. "You're a natural."

I smile. Being with Altagracia doesn't feel familiar, not exactly, but I wonder, just maybe, if I have made my first friend in America.

CON ESO TENGO BASTANTE

After school on Monday, I walk home, satisfied the trip is making more sense each time. The markers are becoming familiar. Even the bland brick facade of our apartment building does not look as foreign to me today. I climb the stairs and open our door. It's tight in the frame, and it makes a barking noise when I force it open. It is the opposite of Altagracia's electronic keypad entry.

"Y entonces que va a hacer?" I hear my mother ask.

I follow her voice to the kitchen, with its brown stove and dingy light from one tiny window.

"Ma, acaba de llegar la Ana," she says into her phone. Of course. The phone.

She thrusts it at me with a sense of mission. "Toma. Habla con la Abuela."

I put the phone against my ear. The familiar voice croons at me from the other end, so crisp she could be next door, so far she could be on Mars. "M'hijita, como te extrañamos." And then she starts to cry.

I want to tell her I miss her too. But it's too big a chunk of words to bite off, and suddenly the Spanish won't come to me. I want to tell her that I made a new friend. That English is revealing itself, slowly and then quickly and then slowly again. That it is hard to hold the pain of missing them and of being here all at once, that I feel guilty that I don't reach out more, but that it doesn't mean I've forgotten them. That keeping them close hurts too much sometimes and it is easier to hold them at a distance. I want to tell her that my mother is so unhappy, that I was sure this was all a mistake, except for sometimes, lately, when I wonder if it could be something beautiful. Maybe.

I look at my mother's hopeful face. How long have they been on the phone? What does she tell her about our life here? Does she pretend to be strong, or does she cry out her loneliness to her mother? Would I tell mine? I have her right in front of me, and I don't.

My mother jerks her chin at me. "Dale, decile algo a la Abuela."

But it all threatens to pull me under, a wave too big to swim through. Why does my mother do this to herself? How can she let her body live in one place but her heart live in another?

"Ma, I have to go to the bathroom," I say, handing her phone back to her. I stride down the hall feeling awful about being so abrupt with my grandmother. I should have made chitchat about school. I should have told her about Altagracia. I should have told her about Mr. T. telling me I was a poet. She would have understood. She used to sit with me down next to el hornito behind her house and read me love poems by Alfonsina Storni or recite "La Profecía" from memory. She loved beautiful words.

Loves, I remind myself. *Loves.*

But I wonder if learning one language doesn't sometimes mean forgetting a little bit of another.

El ayer se borra
Poco a poco
A little bit at a time
For today to shimmer
Yesterday has to fade
Como la neblina.
If the past we carry folded up inside is too heavy
There is no strength for today.
I sit by a stream
Let yesterday pour through my fingers
To wash myself clean
For today.

ONE GOOD THING
ABOUT AMERICA

I wait outside the school library, grinding the ball of one foot into the top of the other through my black flats, waiting for Neo. *Where is he?*

But before I can get too annoyed, Neo turns the corner from the main hall. He's carrying big red-and-white striped boxes of movie popcorn and a bag in which I can see soda cans. He smiles a big, goofy grin.

"We breakfast!" he says a little too loud.

He makes me laugh in spite of myself. "Shh! They'll hear us. No popcorn in library," I say to him.

"Is okay, is okay," he says breezily. I hold open the

door since his hands are full. Instead of trying to sneak in the snack, he strides right to the librarian's desk.

"Neo!" she calls out like a long-lost friend. "You found the microwave."

"I find," he says proudly.

"I have room three all set up for you. The DVD ### # ##. Let me know if you have any trouble with it."

"Thank you." He smiles sweetly. He must be one of those boys grandmothers and store clerks love. School librarians too, apparently.

Once we're in the room, I ask, "How did you get permission to do all this?"

"Library lady nice. Very nice. Spend one summer in Crete, loves Greece. I explain we do this for class." His words are choppy but he sounds more confident than I've heard him before. He puts down the stuff he's carrying and takes a sweeping bow. "Here we are movies."

He hands me a box of popcorn. From the exchange with the librarian, I understand it is not *actual* movie popcorn, though it is in movie popcorn containers.

I point to one. "How?"

He gives me a satisfied smile. "Ways."

He points to the DVD player. "Ready?" I nod. He

takes the tiny remote control and starts the DVD. It's already at the home screen, so he presses Play. Then he points to the light switch. "Okay?" I nod again, and he turns off the light. Very eighties music starts to play.

The scent of popcorn is full of memories of epics and cartoons and friends giggling in the front row of a darkened theater back home. But now it also means this: this unexpected gesture from a boy I barely know.

The movie starts. Slowly. Very slowly. *The Breakfast Club*. A very long shot of the front of a gray school. Classrooms, lockers, pictures, signs. Why are old movies so slow? Nothing happens for, like, ever. Then finally a girl in a nice car whose dad gives her a present before she gets out of the car, which she doesn't seem to appreciate. Other kids arriving at a school, but not as many as should arrive for a full day. The school is empty except for these five. Why are they there? I have looked up every word Mr. T. wrote on the board—princess, brain, jock, rebel, recluse—but didn't google the plot.

"You understand?" Neo asks.

"No," I say.

"Me too," he says in agreement. "Maybe they get

murder? Then solve murder?" he says this almost hopefully, like at least then something would *happen*.

I snort laugh. "Maybe."

The kids on the screen are getting talked to by a guy with the greasy hair of someone you should not trust. They are sitting in a library that sort of looks like the one in this school.

There is no breakfast.

Nothing happens. They sit together. Are they supposed to figure out how to get breakfast? Is that the challenge? They mumble when they talk and I don't catch most of it. This is a talking movie.

Finally Neo says, "Which one . . . are you? Princess? Brain?"

The five different types of kids in the movie. Isn't that how high school is, everyone sorted into neat categories? Back home I knew my category very well, but here I am not in a category. Or maybe I am, to the other kids. To them I am Outsider.

"I don't know," I say. "Recluse, maybe?"

He laughs, like that's a silly thing for me to say. "Back home, I'm the athlete. Brain too, good with school," he says with no hint of self-consciousness. I would have been embarrassed to say that about myself, although I did well in school back home too.

"Lots of boys like angry one, back home," Neo adds.

"Where I'm from too," I say.

"Why you come here, Ana?"

It's only five words but such a big question. So much bigger than my English can hold, so much bigger than my brain can hold sometimes.

I have learned enough English to know the answer is "a better life." It's what teachers say. It's what I heard a lady at the office say when I was waiting for her to photocopy some medical records from back home and she thought I didn't understand what she was saying. "They come here for a better life, I get it, but we have lots of people here without jobs," she said. But "better life" is not quite right. It makes me feel disloyal to my abuela, to Valentina, to my family and friends back home, like somehow my life with them was something that needed bettering. I don't know if it's better here. There's a different word I would choose.

"A bigger life," I say.

"I like," says Neo. If he's here for a bigger life too, he doesn't say.

"What do you miss most about home?" I ask.

He looks away, throws his hand wide. "Too many

things. So much. The . . . how do you call?" He makes a motion and a sound like cracking a nut.

"Nuts?" I say.

"Yes. But big tree! In my family house," he adds. "Also, every summer, very dry. Fire in the hills. Bad, fire, but smell . . ." He trails off. I understand. I miss the smells of home too.

After the movie finishes, we google the plot. They were in school to be punished. This makes me giggle and I do my best to explain it to Neo. I understand why Mr. T. might have wanted us to watch this movie in which nothing happens . . . there's a certain parallel to what we have to do every day, understand the things going on around us without a lot of clues.

We laugh at this and then Neo shrugs. "So we do it again next week? New movie? We ask Mr. T. give us a list and we watch. Okay?"

I smile. "Okay." I study his face, the way it seems open, easy to read.

He says a bunch of things in Greek, catches himself, scrunches up his mouth in frustration. *I know*, I want to say. I know what it's like to want to say more.

"So . . . rule? No Google," he says. "No Google . . . what is word? Before?"

He doesn't want us to google the plot before, but to try to figure it out as we watch. That's what I'm getting, anyway. Even though we were completely lost on this one, maybe we'll start picking up some more as we go along.

"Okay," I say.

"Okay." He nods.

We walk out of the library and past the vending machine near the cafeteria. It is lit up, a beacon of Americanness that always beams its lights and calls me in. Neo turns to it.

"They have food machines in this school. #### ##### ##### ####." He says some things, and I'm not sure if they're Greek or English. It is, as I've heard Mr. T. say, Greek to me. He walks up to the vending machine.

"One last food," he says.

I nod.

He feeds money into the machine. The machine stubbornly refuses his crumpled bills, but with a final gulp, it sucks the last one in. He punches the numbers like someone who has bought from this machine before. We watch as it groans, releasing a box off its ledge. He's chosen candy with pictures of flames on it.

He fishes it out of the bottom, opens it up, holds it out to me. I grab one. The little red nub bursts in my mouth with heat and cinnamon. I smile.

"Is one good thing about America, no?"

I laugh. "Yes. One good thing." But today, I can think of at least one more.

Review of The Breakfast Club

Mr. T:
Thank you for recommending The Breakfast Club.

Our honest review is:
Not enough breakfast
Not enough murders
Not enough words we know.
But we like the dancing
And what they wrote at the end.
We also are rebel, recluse, princess, athlete, brain.
And we add to that poet. And artist. And strangers.

I LIKE YOUR BUNS

The hallway to the cafeteria is all windows. It looks out into a courtyard of trees surrounded by emerald-green grass. The courtyard bursts with ripe, old life, one tree with lemon-yellow leaves, another with juicy orange ones, a bush with dramatic red ones so bright I could see how it might have been the inspiration for the burning bush. Yes, leaves changed back home. But this wild, riotous vegetation that insists upon itself everywhere, in sidewalk cracks and even sprouting from the facades of neglected buildings . . . we didn't have anything like this. The plants had more modesty there. Here, the nature shows off, just like everything else.

I walk into the cafeteria. The volume is turned up to ten, voices going at once, bouncing off the double-height ceiling, bouncing back. I am not a fan of the cafeteria, but I forgot the lunch my mother packed for me.

And so I am clutching the wrinkled dollars from the bottom of my bag, focusing on what I'll need to remember to navigate the line, when I hear, "Hey! Ana!"

I turn. Harrison, in a long-sleeved T-shirt as green as the grass outside, looking ruddy, like he's just been running in cold air, sitting at a table between me and the line to get food. My hands twitch to touch his face. *Stop thinking these things, Ana.*

He's with the girls, the Very American Girls.

"Hello, Harrison," I say.

"I didn't know we have the same lunch. I never see you in here."

I shrug, hoping it looks mysterious. *Wouldn't you like to know what I do at lunch?* Not like I scarf down my mother's sandwiches at the back of a classroom so I won't have to worry about finding someone to sit with, since Altagracia has a different lunch period.

"Where's your food?" he asks.

I point to the line.

"Oh, cool. I was just going to go get seconds. You'll sit with us? Frankie, you can scoot, right?" He nods toward one of the girls sitting at the table beside him.

Frankie regards me coolly. I'm not sure what *scooting* is, but she doesn't look particularly eager to do it.

He's already barreling toward the line, saying something about sausages and heaven. With the background noise, it's even harder than usual to make out what he's saying.

The line moves with surprising efficiency. I take a tiny apple and a sandwich that looks like it's stuffed with mashed-up eggs, which, frankly, mesmerizes me. I don't know anyone who would put mushed-up eggs in a cold sandwich, held together by what looks like mayonnaise, one of my favorite things on earth. Genius.

Harrison leads us back to the table, the scent of his second helping wafting behind him. He got a bunch of pieces of sausage and peppers on a giant bun.

We sit. The girl he called Frankie pushes off to her left to make a space for me, bumping the girl with the sheet of straight black hair and bright-blue eyeshadow. They're the ones from math class. Harrison sits across from me, and another girl I recognize sits to his right.

"You know everyone?" asks Harrison, taking a

giant bite of his sausage sandwich. I think of this word, "sandwich," so like the Spanish word, "sánguche." Which language had it first? Where does it come from?

I don't share any of these thoughts, because they race through my head all day long, and if I said them every time I think them, no one would ever sit next to me again. I give my head a small shake in response to his question, like maybe we can skip this part if I just don't move that much.

The girl next to me says, "No, ######, just because you know someone doesn't ##### we just ###### ######, like through the ###### ###### of knowing people." Her bangs are severe and she's penciled in her eyebrows dark and sharp, giving her an intense look. But her eyes are smiling. "I'm Frankie," she says. "Francesca, but can you even? So, no, Frankie."

The other girl leans in and smiles. "Britt." She's wearing a sports uniform and has the knobby fingers of someone who is rough on her hands.

The one across from her says, "Hey. Jessica." She's got smart eyes, like someone who can size you up just by looking at you. Her wavy, honey-colored hair looks like it took hours to get photo-ready. I wonder if she knows Altagracia.

"Why so formal, Jess?" says Harrison, catching a bit of sausage grease with a napkin. "I haven't heard you introduce yourself as Jessica since the third grade."

Jessica doesn't reply and the silence between us feels dense. Even the cafeteria noise seems to die down a little.

I want to say something. Fill the silence. "You like . . ." I wave my hand at Harrison's sandwich. There's another word I think I learned for it, something that is supposed to go with sausage. It's not a sandwich exactly, but . . . what's the word? Mr. T. taught it to us just the other day during the "American food" class. I start again. "I like the . . . buns? And sausage?"

Frankie, Britt, and Jessica look at each other, then burst out laughing. Were those the wrong words? I look at their faces, red with laughter, and then it comes to me, where else I have heard "buns." Looking at the sausage, I can only guess what it means, too.

I want to melt into the tile.

Harrison frowns at them. "Don't mind them. All those volleyballs to the head," he says. "I like this bun very much, as a matter of fact. A fine sourdough bun. And the sausage and peppers are truly excellent."

Frankie says, "Hey, sorry, it was just the look on his face. That's what we were laughing at."

Jessica narrows her eyes at me, ignoring Frankie's attempt to make it less awkward. "I saw you on Gracie's Instagram. Interesting thing she did to your lips there." Her tone says she did not really think it was interesting.

"I know!" says Britt sincerely. "Truly, that girl is a magician. And I mean . . . you! You looked amazing."

Jessica makes just the subtlest arch of her eyebrows.

"I ##### ####### lipstick on for longer than twenty minutes," says Frankie.

"You should probably stop kissing so many people then," says Jessica, eyebrow still arched. Maybe she's just like that with everyone.

Frankie puts her hand on my upper arm. "We weren't laughing at you, about the buns thing, really. I'm sorry. It was just, he just froze, and this goofball has the silliest face." Harrison throws a fry at her. She goes on. "Your accent is cute, it really is. And . . . I think it's really brave ###### ###### #####. Coming to a whole other country."

Britt leans in again so I can see her behind Frankie. "Me too. My grandparents are immigrants, and ##### ########. I hope we weren't #### #######."

"No," I say. "It's okay."

Jessica pointedly doesn't say anything.

Harrison clears his throat. "My parents and I went to Italy last summer, and in the cities it was fine because everyone spoke English, but when we went out into the countryside for a few days, literally I did not know how to ask for a slice of bread. It was so ##############. Is that what it's like for you here every day?"

I smile. He is trying to imagine what it might be like for me. And that is sweet. But I wonder if he really thinks that being on a fancy trip for a few days is the same as leaving behind nearly everyone and every place you've ever loved.

"I can ask for bread," I say. Then I lift one shoulder in a little shrug. "But buns are more of a problem."

And this time when they laugh, I laugh with them.

Recipe for Disaster

How do you get an apple in your eye?
Just how easy is pie?
Who would eat crow or eat their heart out?
Or how could anyone eat enough hay to eat like a
horse?
How can a potato sit on the couch?
In a world where so many things are confusing,
even food,
I dream of a day when it is a piece of cake.

WHEN YOU FINALLY KNOW THE WAY

Neo and I have picked Wednesdays for our continuing movie series. Mr. T. liked our idea and gave us a list of movies long enough to get us through the year. Today's installment is *Sixteen Candles*. I have kept my promise not to google it, but it doesn't take a genius to figure out it's about someone's sixteenth birthday, which I like, since that's how old I am. I told Neo that I'd bring the snacks today, and I grab a container full of the sugar cookies my mom helped me make. I hope I can get them out of the container fast enough for Neo not to notice my mother's habit of reusing plastic containers that food came in—this one used to be a giant tub of ice cream—instead of the specially made plastic containers kids use for their lunches.

I quickly unpack the cookies and stash the container under my sweater. Neo comes in and gobbles down four cookies so fast I'm pretty sure he must have eaten two at a time. "Oreah," he says, or at least I think that's what he says. He swallows. "Sorry," he says again. "Hungry."

About fifteen minutes into the movie, he says to me, "This family is terrible, no?" I nod. "They make the wedding the day after the girl's birthday? What family would do this thing? Only Americans would care so little about family."

I was wondering the same thing. Couldn't they have made the sister's wedding a different day, not so close to the girl's birthday? Did no one notice when they planned it?

I pause the movie, but accidentally hit the menu button. I click around a little . . . Spanish subtitles! That could help a lot.

I say to Neo, "Look. What it says, written down, but in Spanish."

"Greek?" he asks hopefully. Maybe we can take turns having the subtitles in Spanish and in Greek.

I click around. No Greek.

"I tell you the Spanish and we put into translation app. Only for the stuff you really want to know."

He scrunches his mouth skeptically. "This is . . . what is the word? Cheating?"

"It's not like googling," I say in my most persuasive voice. "It's just for helping us understand."

"Okay," he grants me, sounding reluctant.

The subtitles help a little, but they don't make the movie any less weird. Is this how things are in the United States? Or how things used to be? Because there's an Asian character that is like a cartoon character, not an actual person. And . . . did the boys say this other, much younger boy needed to get the main character's panties? Eww.

We stop to plug the Spanish into the app to get the Greek. Neo makes a horrified face, then bursts out laughing. I have no idea what the app spit out in Greek, but it can't be good.

"Silly old movie. I do not like this underwear thing. No respect."

I laugh. We're from two very different places, but we have a lot in common. Talking to Neo is not easy, since there are so many words lost between us, but still it feels like a cool breeze after a long, hot day.

As we watch further into the movie and it becomes

obvious that the guy she has a crush on also seems to like her too, it makes me wonder out loud, "Why does this boy just not talk to her?"

Neo studies the back of the chair to his right. "I don't know."

It finishes, and the ending is sweet. She does get together with the cute guy, in a shot I remember seeing a poster of somewhere, her hair up, a birthday cake full of candles between them.

Neo pops the last cookie in his mouth. "One more?" he asks. I look at the empty plate of cookies. I shrug. *No. No more.*

"Movie. One more movie," he explains.

I don't want to look at the time, because there's something warm about picking my way through a history of teen movies with this boy who is as lost as I am. It will mean getting home later than I'm supposed to. "Yes," I say.

He pulls out Mr. T.'s list. "Warning, next one is weird."

"How do you know?" I ask.

"It says right in the title."

I smile. "What can be weirder than this one?" I ask. He nods, and goes off to get the DVD.

Neo and I say goodbye at the library door. He heads in the direction opposite of the door I use. I go outside. The buses are all gone. Duh. Of course all the buses are gone. I text my mom, but she doesn't reply, which is weird. I don't try my dad, because if he's working I'd feel bad pulling him away from a paying ride.

I walk home. The air is clear, crisp, alive. The leaves pool luxuriously around my feet, and a breeze skitters them. It's like a carpet of so many colors, and I kick them up with my steps. I glance around to make sure no one is looking, then jump in a giant pile by the side of the road. I sink in hip-deep. What a place where there are so many leaves! Where do they put them all?

It's a long walk but I don't mind it. I am filled with a bubbling sense of joy . . . I know the way now. These streets used to feel like unfriendly, anonymous mazes. Now the next turn presents itself in my memory: Right onto Palmer. Left onto Highwood. I marvel at the realization. Somewhere in my brain, when I wasn't paying attention, I learned the way.

BUEN ANIVERSARIO

I climb the stairs to my apartment, shake off bits of dried leaves stuck to my leggings and the furry top of my boots. The hallway is filled with a familiar, friendly scent: picadillo. Chopped meat, onions, and red pepper. I've made it with my mom and grandmother so many times, usually in preparation for a holiday or a big family dinner. Before I open the door, I hear the music: Charles Aznavour sings in Spanish. Old-timey music from before my own parents were born, but which they've always loved for some reason. I am intruding. I almost feel like I should knock.

In the kitchen, my mother is swaying to the music,

a bright-yellow apron tied around her dress. *She's in a dress. She's wearing makeup.* My father is holding a glass of dark-red wine. They're laughing to a private joke before they realize I'm standing in the doorway.

My mother turns to me. Her eyes are bright.

"M'hijita! There you are! Where have you been?" she says. There's no accusation in the question, only delight.

"I was . . . in the library." It's not the full story, but it is technically true.

"That's my girl, studying hard. Keeping up with the math?" my father asks.

I nod. Also technically true.

"Math is the key in this country. Numbers."

I nod again.

"Come on, sit with us. Get a soda," he says. He tips his glass of wine at me. I go in the fridge and pour myself a glass of Sprite.

The song changes to the next one, one about an anniversary where everything is going wrong. *Oh, of course. Their anniversary.* "Yo cumplo mi deber, yo debo de callar," Aznavour trills out with background music that sounds slightly like a 1960s caper movie in which a sophisticated safe-cracking should be happening. *I had completely forgotten.* It's strange for their anniversary to be on this cold day full of early darkness. It's spring back home. They were married in the spring. I remember spying them slow dancing to this song when I was little, his hand on the small of her back. She walks over to him with a wooden spoon full of picadillo for him to taste. He does, and smiles at her, glowing. "It just gets better every time."

I smile wide and full, cracked open with joy that my parents are still inside the shells they've been wearing.

"See? We don't need that social club," my dad says.

"What social club?" I ask.

"Eh, just a bunch of old-timers. Drinking wine and talking about back home."

I consider telling him that from where I sit he's an old-timer drinking wine, but, in his defense, he's not talking about back home. He's just trying to remake it.

"I didn't know there was a social club," I say.

"El mundo es un pañuelo," my mom says brightly. My father doesn't object to her Spanish, maybe because he likes the saying. *The world is a handkerchief. Small, so small, like something you can hold in your hand.* Maybe that feels cozier to him.

He explains an old neighbor from back home has a son who lives not far away from here. When the old neighbor and one of my aunts were comparing notes about where in the US their families live, they made the connection. My aunt told my mom about the social club. "Asados once a month and the men watch fútbol," my mom explains.

"We're in America now. We don't need to get together with a bunch of people just wishing for the past. We have our own social club right here," my dad replies, beaming at her. He's his old self. His eyes say he loves her. "Dale, mi amor," he says, slipping on the Spanish himself. "Put the lid on that picadillo for a minute y baila conmigo. Let's dance."

I slip off to my bedroom to let them dance alone. I used to think it was gross to see my parents love each other. But now it feels reassuring, like a thing I thought I'd forgotten to pack but found at the bottom of the suitcase weeks later.

As long as I don't have to watch.

I call Valentina. She picks up.

"We practice English." She smiles. *Oh no, another one.* I want to tell her I have plenty of that here, but I know she's been working on it for when she visits me.

Her cat jumps up on her lap.

"¡Pompón!" I squeal. I haven't seen him in all the times Valentina and I have talked.

She puts a tiny feathered hat on Pompón. "Now he is glamorous like American. Like you," she jokes. I smile.

It is good to see her looking so happy. She's put foundation over her freckles, something I've never seen her do before. But of course she'll be changing without me too, now.

COUNTING ON IT

I'm about two blocks away from school. Now that I realize I know the way, I kind of like the walk, even in the morning. The air is like the blast from a refrigerator when you first open it, fresh, hopeful.

I have my music cranked up on the earbuds my dad splurged on for me. It gives a rhythm to my walk.

But now I'm in my own world, which is why I don't hear Harrison until he's two steps ahead of me. He's wearing a burgundy school hoodie and his hair looks like he left the house without running a comb through it, which is not a bad look for him. He's smiling like he's bananas, and walking backward.

I take out one of my earbuds.

"You didn't hear anything I just said," he says.

"Nope." I smile.

"I said, 'whatcha listening to?'"

"Oh!" I don't actually know the name of the band. It's a playlist I found the other day. I'm also not sure how to explain all that. I take out an earbud, hand it to him. His face lights up.

"I don't know these guys. They're ###### good."

I like that I am able to show him something he doesn't know, since it feels like he's got the whole handbook for everything *Here* and I am only *There*.

He starts bopping his head to the beat. "You hear that bass there? That's some good bass."

"You like music a lot?" I ask. It's not exactly what I want to ask, but it's close enough.

"Yeah. It started with music lessons I ###### ########### #### when I was a kid. Violin in kindergarten #########. Then I ##### piano. Finally ####### guitar, I wanna say like in eighth grade, when #### ###### cool for that." He smiles sheepishly. "So what all this means is that I'm mediocre at several instruments."

"Mediocre?" I ask. It reminds me of a Spanish word.

All the same letters, but way different pronunciation.

"Like, so-so. Okay." He motions with his hands, the "not so great" wobble that looks like it means the same thing here as it does back home. I laugh, remembering Altagracia calling Harrison soso. So *so* cute, maybe.

"I'm in a band," he goes on. "Vocals, mostly. ##### ##### guitar sometimes, but nobody needs ####### that."

I want to ask him more, but he keeps going before I can say anything else.

"Anyway, #### mom is going to kill me and ######## ######### musical fame and fortune if I don't do something about math this year. I don't know what it is, ####### ##### ########! But I am really struggling. Like . . . wasn't that test completely indecipherable the other day?"

Indecipherable. I sound it out in my head. I know "in" means opposite, and it sounds like the word for "number" is in there, cifra. So something about the numbers being opposite? Wrong? Something about not understanding. Harrison found the math test indecipherable the way I find so many things here, I guess.

I look ahead. I got a ninety-eight on that test, but it seems impolite to say.

"Oh, man, you did okay on the test, didn't you?" he asks, reading my face.

"I did okay."

"Now you've gotta tell me. Okay, I'll tell you. I got a sixty-two. My mother is going to ######### complete freak-out ##### ####. Cs are a problem at my house and failing is seriously not an option."

"I did not get a sixty-two on the test," I say. Which is true.

"Seventy?"

I smile. He really wants to know. "Higher."

"Oh man, you are putting me to shame here. Eighty?"

"If you do all the homework carefully that will pull up your grade. It's not all about the tests."

"The homework is impossible too. Ninety?"

"Ninety-eight," I say finally.

He grasps his chest like he's just been hit by an arrow, pantomimes trying to pull it out, staggers backward, pretends to die against a tree. I smile but keep walking. He catches back up.

"If she was ever planning on grading on a curve,

you just screwed a whole lot of people," he says, but I can tell from his smile he is only joking.

"I'm sorry," I say. I'm not that sorry.

He jumps in front of me again. The music is still playing on the earbud, and he dances to it wacky, all arms. "I have an idea how you can make it up to me."

We're almost at school now. A pack of sports guys walks up the steps carrying sticks for a sport I don't recognize. A girl kicks up the skateboard she just rode in with, tucks it under her arm, flicks bangs out of her eyes. I wonder what it feels like to be that effortless. I think maybe I was, once, back home. Except I just didn't know it.

"How?"

"I think you should tutor me."

I turn to face Harrison now. "I . . . what? How?"

"What do you mean, how? You show me how the problems are done. I do them. You point out why I'm a dumbass."

I can think of several thousands of reasons why this probably makes no sense. Like the thousands of words I would need to explain math to him but don't know. But I can think of one very good reason why it's a great idea, starting with the way Harrison sometimes bites his lip when he's deep in concentration. And how his fingers move when he's holding a pencil and doing problems. And . . .

"Okay," I say. "I can help."

He jumps straight up three times, incredibly high each time. We're at the foot of the steps to the school. He hands me my earbud. "When I'm playing Madison Square Garden, I'll give you a shout-out for preventing my mother from locking me in my room for math-related reasons."

I laugh. "I'll count on it."

The Math of You

Tú eres una cifra
I can't add or subtract
Un problema I can't factor
A presence I want to multiply
You're a prime number
Maybe one of those problems with no solution
and the math of you makes so much sense to me
right now

NO TODO EL MONTE
ES ORÉGANO

After school, I'm at my locker stuffing it with text-books that don't want to fit. Altagracia pops up next to me, looking video-ready as always. Her hair is piled on her crown, and she's got a subtle pink eyeshadow on that makes her eyes look a different color than they usually do. She's in a white tracksuit with a cropped, belly-baring zip-up top trimmed in silver.

"What would you say to a dinner date tonight?"

"Dinner?"

"It's kind of an emergency."

"An emergency dinner?"

"My dad wants me to play nice with his girlfriend."

"Decile que no." I tell her. "Can't you say no?"

"Bonding, blah blah, this one's the one, blah blah. So . . . will you come?"

"How will I help, if I come?"

Altagracia clears her throat, pretending to toss her hair over her shoulder and putting on an overly formal accent: "Oh, Altos Gracios, your father tells me you're quite the internet mogul. My cousin/aunt/best friend/college roommate works for Macy's/Sephora/Aunt Ginny's Makeup Blog. I could hook you up!"

I laugh.

"Save me from the horror that is my father's love life!"

"I don't . . ."

"My father has incredibly expensive taste in restaurants. Does that help?"

I scrunch up my nose. "Not really. It's just that my mom . . ." I'm going to say that my mom doesn't love me hanging out with people she doesn't know, which is true, but as soon as I consider saying it I realize it makes me sound like a second grader.

"Oh, overprotective parent? No problem. I've got one of those, although luckily she's in another country. So . . . get Mom on the phone."

"What?"

"Yeah, I'm serious. Parents love me."

I look at her hair, the shave on the side. I'm not sure she's met parents like mine.

"Come on. Please. I wanna meet Mom."

I laugh, take out my phone, dial my mom. When she picks up, I explain the situation. I don't do it very well, because Altagracia keeps making faces at me, signaling for me to hand her the phone.

"Hola, Ma!" Altagracia yells toward the phone.

"Dejame hablar con ella," my mom tells me.

"Mrs. Mom," says Altagracia as soon as I hand her the phone. "Sorry, cómo se llama?" Her disarming smile sounds like it crackles on the phone. I wonder what my mom thinks.

"Le explico," says Altagracia. She goes on to explain the situation to my mom. She offers her father's phone number and says the name of a restaurant I'm sure my mother's never heard of. Then she invites my mom to come too! I can hear my mother laughing. The mix of boldness and sweetness has worked. Altagracia hands me the phone again.

"Qué lindo que tenés una amiga así," says my mom. She's happy I have a friend like Altagracia.

I'm happy to have a friend like Altagracia, too.

A good day

When you didn't know you needed a
Parent-whispering
Dad-girlfriend-avoiding
Old-lady-driving
Green-fingernailed
makeup-genius friend
Who can make you laugh at anything
But you're lucky enough to find her anyway.

YOU'RE NOT ALLOWED
TO TALK ALOUD

"So you see here? If you solve for this, then the formula works."

Harrison squints his eyes at it. I check the time on my phone. I'm not sure how long it's been, and I told Neo I'd meet him here for our movie after I tutor Harrison. We've been at it for nearly an hour, and he's better, but not fully there yet.

I find him very distracting. The slight smell of something soapy, the perfect fingernails. If I'm honest, I'm only hearing him in stretches, like when he's asking me a question. But after I scratch out the problem with my pencil, and then he starts to write too, I go somewhere. Somewhere to tight-throat/ shallow-breath land. Somewhere to ohmygodthatcurl-byhisear land. Somewhere else. I wonder if he notices.

I watch him. His eyelashes shift a millimeter at a time as he scans the page, in little jumps, not one smooth glide. His shampoo . . . is that lemon? Would it be weird if I asked him about his shampoo?

Yes, it would be weird.

"So like that, you mean?" he asks, his eyes serious. I look down. I have not been paying attention. I check his work. He missed one step, and it messed the whole thing up. I show him.

He puts down his pencil. He takes a deep breath, laces his fingers behind his head, and stretches his elbows back. I watch his chest move with the inhale. We've been working hard, and I can see he is near the end of his attention too. "You may have gotten your-self into an ######## struggle here, Ana."

I shake my head. "No. I don't think so. With math, there is only one answer. Wrong. Right. Not like English. You want something impossible? Try English."

"I always hear that, but what's hard about English? I take French, and that language was designed to injure your tongue."

I laugh. "Are you serious?"

"You sound like you're doing okay."

I lack precisely the thing to explain what I lack. The words. For every word I get out, there's a whole iceberg of thoughts and hopes and feelings that stay unspoken. But how do I speak them?

"It is very hard."

"Give me one example," he says.

I close my eyes. There's always a river of *what?* that I'm swimming in. How to grab a branch, pick just one thing?

"The machine that makes the noise that wakes you up."

"The alarm?"

"Yes. What does it do?"

"The alarm? It rings."

I sigh. "The other way you say that."

"The alarm . . . goes off?"

"Yes. Off what? The alarm goes on, no?"

He laughs. "I mean, isn't it that way in Spanish?"

"No. La alarma suena. It sounds. It doesn't go off anything. Also, the other day, my teacher said someone passed a test 'by the skin of his teeth.' Besides how disgusting that sounds, teeth don't have skin?"

He laughs again.

I'm on a roll. "And another thing. What is the sound of the first letter of the alphabet?"

"A? A."

"Is it? How do you say P-A-N-I-C?"

"I guess then it would be pay-nic," he says, smiling.

"There are so many ways to say A. Ah, eh, ay. You know how many ways in my language? One." This is probably one of the hardest things about English, how each vowel could be pronounced a bunch of different ways and just when you think you've learned them all, you hear another one, or the exception to a rule.

We keep going on about the difficulty of the English language and I can't believe how many examples I have to share. There is everything from "always" to "all ways" and "whack" to "wack," which seems to mean uncool. "Or how about this? You are not *allowed* to talk *aloud* in the library."

Harrison tips his chair back and falls to the carpet on purpose. His messy hair falls behind him on the orange wall-to-wall carpeting. "You win. I am slain," he says, hands on his heart.

I want to jump on top of him. He is just so cute. I look around. Is it okay that we're making this scene in the library? I guess you are *allowed* to talk *aloud* in the library after all. If I did jump on him, would anyone see?

I look toward the door.

Yes. One person would see.

Neo.

Neo is standing in the doorway.

His eyes travel from me to Harrison on the floor with his hands over his heart. He's here for our movie. I must have lost track of time. I feel a strange twinge, like I lied. I told him I was coming here to study. And I was. But . . . well, obviously we are not studying now.

But why should it matter if we had a little fun at the end of studying?

I extend my hand down to Harrison to help him get up off the floor. He takes it, hops up, then follows my line of sight to Neo. "Oh, is this your next . . . study thing?" He is back to being serious now, in one sudden moment.

"Yes," I say.

"You . . . okay, that's cool. Tuesday, then?" I nod. Harrison picks up his stuff, puts it in his backpack.

"Okay, well, see you," I say awkwardly as I head to the AV room with Neo. It's a thick silence, with a swirl to it.

"You study different math than I study," he says.

There's a bite to the statement, a little like an accusation.

"We were just . . ."

He waves his hand at me. "No, no, sorry. Bad day today."

"I'm sorry. Do you want to do this another day?"

He shakes his head slowly again, breaks the gaze. "No, let's watch the movie."

And we do, but it's not like other times. We both have our minds on something else.

POTLUCK

It smells like empanadas.

That happens like this: the right kind of meat from the best butcher you can find. That was a little hard this time around, since we don't know the best butcher. But still, my mom used her special meat-choosing powers to pick the right ones: a cut of churrasco, then another one that in English they called "chuck" (which I think is a man's name too?), plus another one with plenty of fat. Then home, cut the meat in two-centimeter cubes, put them into the brand-new meat grinder, once, then twice. It's funny to see a shiny meat grinder and not the ancient one that three generations of hands from my mother's family had washed. But this one works fine.

The chopped-up yellow onions are simmered until they're see-through. Then you add the meat, and the whole thing is cooked over the stove. It makes the entire place smell like the best thing anywhere: the meat, plus yellow onions, plus red pepper flakes, plus salt. It occurs to me that someday I may need to know how to make this on my own, so I ask my mother every time, "But how do you know how much salt?"

"You watch," she says. Which is no answer at all.

The picadillo is put into the fridge overnight. When it's cold and hard, the meat filling is easier to scoop into the dough. This made it hard back home at the high heat of Christmas, when you were racing against the balmy air to stuff all the empanadas before the juice ran and made closing them impossible. Which makes me wonder: What will it be like for it to be cold at Christmas, like in all the American Christmas movies we watched? Is everything really covered with snow?

My mother and I carry out our usual tasks, the same thing I have done since I was four years old. She rolls out the dough she's made by hand paper thin. She scoops out a tablespoon of filling. On each, I put one small piece of hard-boiled egg and one pitted olive.

When I was small, the olives used to have pits, and then you could count how many empanadas each person had eaten by the pits on their plates. Then she wets one side of the dough, folds the other side over, cuts around it with a pizza cutter, and makes a magic little braid thing to seal it up, lightning quick, which I've tried a hundred times to make but just can't. Then it's my job to put them on the baking sheet and paint them with egg, which she's beat, her hands moving like a blur.

This is one of my favorite things to do. This says Christmas. It says birthdays. It says my aunts laughing around the kitchen table, telling stories of old unfortunate endings and boys who came to see them on bicycles, of dances and angry mothers waving rolling pins.

And now, it says ESL potluck.

Potluck. This is a new word. I had to look it up when Mr. T. suggested we all bring in something from our home countries to share with each other. I instantly loved this word: potluck. We did parties like this back home, too, but we didn't have this fantastic word. Where could such wonderfulness possibly come from? I imagine ancient people believing that all the different pots brought luck. I hope that's what it is, and I hope it's true.

"Ana, so explain it again. Altagracia's father did what now?"

"Se enamora muy rápido, dice Altagracia." *He falls in love very fast.* "Pero se le pasa pronto también. That woman from the other day?" I make the *pfft* sign across the neck of "over." The woman Altagracia's dad had been dating has already moved into the "ex" category.

She laughs. She met my father when she was fourteen. All of her sisters and all of her friends did a similar thing. "You said he has that big house. Maybe money makes you do weird things." She giggles.

"¿Qué excusa tenemos nosotros?" I smile at her.

She swats at me with cloth she's got at her left side to wipe her hands free of the flour she uses to keep the dough from sticking to her hands. "Ay, Ana," she says in mock anger. Then she adds, "Contame de la escuela. ¿Los chicos están lindos?"

"There are no boys," I say. I know better than to talk to my mom about this. For women who met their husbands at fourteen and stuck to them, there's very little room for just liking someone. You do not bring a boy home until you're sure he's "the one." And how you ever know such a thing, I can't even imagine.

"¿Así que tu escuela es solo para chicas?"

I roll my eyes at her. "No, my school is *not* just for girls. I mean, there's no boy that . . ." I don't want to lie.

She reads me instantly. "¡Te gusta un chico! ¿Un americanito?"

She always sees right through me in some creepy, almost unnatural way. It's always impossible for me to keep secrets from her. When I was little I used to ask her how she knew everything and she'd laugh and say, "I just do." When she was mad, she'd say, "Mientras tú vas, yo vuelvo." *While you're on your way there, I'm on my way back.* I look at her. She's rosy from the heat in the kitchen, with floury hands and a strand of hair escaping her ponytail. She looks like . . . herself. She looks happy. I nod.

"Handsome? Tall?" She thinks all American men are handsome and tall, like in commercials.

Except in this case, she happens to be right, so I nod again.

"Cuidado, Ana," she says sweetly, but just sharply enough for me to remember we're on slightly different teams. *Careful.* It makes me pull back just a millimeter.

"We're friends, Ma," I say. "Amigos, no más." To her credit, she doesn't push for more.

There's not much more to tell, honestly. Harrison and I have been getting together a few times a week after school. And he's been doing better in math, turning in every homework assignment, getting solid grades on quizzes and tests. Once we met in the music room to study, after all the band kids had cleared away, and he played me a song on a guitar. He has a beautiful, deep singing voice. I don't think I was much help in math after that, with my heart thudding in my ears the whole time.

Neo and I have made progress on the list of movies, too, but it's been quiet, different from before.

My mother clears her throat. She's made six empanadas on a long stretch of dough, and she's waiting for me to put the olive and egg on each of them. I scramble to do my part. She playfully folds and cuts as if chasing me.

I study my mother again. It is still strange to see her here sometimes, like someone plucked her out of one TV show where she belongs and stuck her in the wrong one. But today is different.

Today, for once, she looks at home.

ALBÓNDIGAS BY ANY
OTHER NAME

On potluck day, Neo and I go to the refrigerator where the lunch ladies have let us store our dishes before going to class. Neo carries a big ceramic dish full of little cylinders of what looks like meat.

"Albóndigas?" I ask, pointing to the dish. I'm hoping the word in Greek sounds similar enough to the Spanish so that he'll understand, because I don't know the word in English. In hearing him trying to explain things to me, I've caught a few words that are almost the same in Greek and Spanish: pantalones, for one.

"Kefthedes," he replies, like the answer should have been obvious. So, no, not albóndigas.

"Can I?" I ask. I know we're supposed to wait, but they look delicious.

He nods. I pull up the plastic wrap, pop a whole one in my mouth. It *is* an albóndiga, by another name, with a little more of an herb taste than the ones my mother makes. So it's an albóndiga, but it's also . . . not?

"What's in it?" I ask.

He puffs up a little in that way of his when he's about to tell me something about his culture, his home. "Meat. Potato. Bread. No, no bread . . . in the . . ." He makes a gesture with his fingers. The little pieces that fall off bread . . . I don't know the word for that either.

I give him one empanada, which he gobbles up in two bites. We head toward the ESL class.

The boy with the army-short hair—the one who picked on Neo that first month of school—is standing with his back on a locker, facing the door of the ESL classroom. Today he's in camouflage pants and a different skintight shirt. The muscle in his jaw jumps as he watches us coming down the hall. He leans over to a shorter buddy and says something without taking his eyes off us, gesturing toward us with his chin.

Neo walks in front of me. I can't tell from the back of him if he's getting the same feeling I am. I don't know the right words to warn him.

As we get close to the door, the boy takes one step forward. "Fucking ESL classes now. I guess we didn't build that wall fast enough," he says, looking at me dead in the eye.

Neo stops walking.

"It's okay," I whisper at his back. "Just go in the class."

Neo takes a halting step forward, like he's deciding. The boy gives his plate a nudge, playing at upending it. For a sickening second I think Neo may drop it and hit the guy. The guy's friends all have eyes on us, like they want to see this play out.

"Move," I say, in the strongest way I know how. I hope it *sounds* strong, because my elbows are turning to jelly and my heart is threatening to run away.

"Oh, look, your girlfriend just got here and she already thinks she owns the joint, huh?"

Still Neo doesn't step forward toward the door.

"They're stupid," I say. "Let's go in." The boy reaches for the plate again. Neo jerks it away. A few kefthedes slip out the side and tumble to the floor. The friends find this hilarious.

"Oh, you wanna come and take welfare but you don't want to share?" His friends give another grumbly laugh. He's doing this for an audience.

My throat is full of something that won't go down. I hoist my tray of empanadas under my left arm and reach around Neo to open the door. Mr. T. is right inside.

"Come on," I say urgently. "Just go in."

Mr. T. looks at my face, then at the boys behind me, already dispersing. "Everything okay?" This pulls Neo into the classroom.

I walk over to the table, which is piled with delicious-looking plates. The table doesn't match the swirl of ugliness right outside it.

We put our stuff down. I take Neo's wrist so that he'll look at me. "You okay? Don't listen to those jerks." I don't know that I'm following my own advice, because I can still feel the hate coming from the hall. How can people think they know anything about us just because we're in this class?

His face is full of something I can't read. "I'm okay," he says. But he puts a hand on his middle . . . in the back and forth, some grease from the bottom of his pan spilled all down the front of his shirt.

Mr. T. pops his head between us, spots the grease. "Oh no! Hey, c'mere, I've got a stash of T-shirts. #### ##### ### #### ##." He takes the first one from the pile, holds it up to Neo. It has a band name on it, with flames looking like they're about to consume the letters. I'm not sure what it means, but the flames seem to fit the occasion.

Neo goes in the corner and turns his back to the class. He pulls off his shirt in one smooth motion and I'm surprised to see how strong his back looks. It is tanned and freckled from the sun, almost as though he left Greece weeks ago, not months. He pulls on the new shirt, and I dart my eyes away before he sees I've been staring.

Mr. T. pops one of Neo's albóndigas in his mouth. "Mmm, I just love meatballs," he says.

Meat.

Balls.

Sometimes English does just tell it like it is.

We serve ourselves a plate of everything. Mr. T. walks around and puts a bit of reddish jelly on the turkey. It's the berry sauce, and it is just as strange as it sounds. But everything else is fantastic—mashed potatoes, corn, plus other tasty dishes from my classmates. The empanadas are a big hit, although I didn't realize that Adira is a vegetarian, which I feel bad about not having known. I save one for Altagracia. She's always teasing me about how Dominican empanadas are way better than ours and promising to take me to her favorite Dominican place the next town over.

"Okay, so Thanksgiving. Unfortunately a lot of what you're going to learn about Thanksgiving in history is going to be bullshit. Don't tell them I said that, sorry," Mr. T. says to the intercom, like it's listening. "But ##### ## #### we can also make things our own. So, a day to be together with people ######## #### think about why we're grateful . . . that's not so bad. So I'll start."

We all wait, the sound of forks scraping paper plates dying down.

"I . . . look, I'm going to be honest. I wasn't sure why they assigned me this class. I barely speak one language, let alone all the ones that you guys speak. #### ### ####. ### #### ##. But you guys . . ." He trails off, looks at the board for a second. "The courage you guys have. How hard you try. It's inspiring. I'm grateful for that. And I hope I'm worthy of being your teacher."

I feel like maybe we should clap? But no one says anything, or moves to do it, so I just look at him like everyone else.

"Okay, anyway," says Mr. T., shaking the moment away. "When I was growing up, my parents ###

making us each say a thing we're grateful for. I just gave you mine. Now you guys."

One by one the class shares what they are thankful for: Adira says her family, even her little sister, who gets on her nerves sometimes. Wati says his new friend. Soo says her new roller skates. Bhagatveer makes everyone laugh when he earnestly thanks his new Xbox.

"Neo?" prompts Mr. T.

"I am grateful for . . . American movies," he says. He looks at me briefly, then at the floor and away. His mood seems to have brightened since the ugliness in the hall.

"Oh, good! I love that. Ana?"

I have been searching my brain for an answer since he started going around the room. Some of the other answers resonate for me too. I am grateful that in this world of swirling forces, at least my immediate family is together. I am glad that everyone I love is safe, even if some of them are far away. I feel strong and, most days, up to the challenge before me. But I want to reach inside and find something more to say.

And then I have it.

"I am grateful for every new word." I smile.

The bell rings, and Mr. T. appears at my desk.

"Ana, I've been meaning to talk to you," he says. "This literary magazine I subscribe to . . . They're doing a poetry contest. For high school students. And I think you should enter."

My eyes widen. "Me?" I look behind Mr. T. and see Neo watching us.

"Yes! You're very talented, Ana. The world should get to read your poetry." Mr. T. smiles. "Just think about it. Okay?"

I nod. It's hard to imagine. Me? With my brand-new English poems? But I don't want to disappoint Mr. T.

"I will think about it," I say.

A voice does not equal the courage to use it
Words do not equal something to say
Añoro can mix with a dream for the future
A dance of what's lost and what's yet to be found
In the forest of words I search for the answers
In the river of silence I search for the sound
On the cliff I look out on all that surrounds me
For the whispers I've hidden and my voice yet
unbound.

THE GIRL WITH ALL THE WORDS

I am sitting in the library for a free period when Neo strolls in. He is not usually here during this time, not that I've ever seen before. He seems surprised to see me too.

He walks bouncily, like he just won something, so it surprises me when he sits across from me and says, "I forgot my gym clothes."

"This is . . . good?"

"Gym is boring here."

"But won't you get in trouble?" I ask.

He shakes his head. "Sanders," he says. It's one word that explains everything. Even I know that if you have Sanders for gym, you can do whatever you want.

"So why did you come to the library?" I ask.

He reaches in his backpack and pulls out a notebook. I've seen this notebook on his desk before. It's spiral-bound and has a beige cover with a line drawing of a building at an angle on it.

"What's that?" I ask.

He flips it open to the first page. "How you say? Building? Beautiful building." I look down at the open page. It's a meticulous drawing of a building that looks familiar a little, skinny on the corner, almost like a slice of cake.

"That's beautiful. You did that?"

He shrugs, as if to push away the compliment. "Not so good. Only copy."

I ask if I can look at it and he pushes it in my direction. The detail is incredible. He's penciled in every window, every shadow beneath the ledges, even a sprig of a plant growing in a crevice in the facade on the first floor. He gets up, goes to a nearby stack, comes back with a book. *Understanding Architecture.*

"Free periods, I come to library, I copy buildings.

One day I make my own buildings."

I remember now. He told me way back at the start of school. He wants to be an architect.

I make a page-flipping motion at the edge of the notebook. "Okay if I look?" I ask.

He looks at me nervously, but after a long beat, he nods. I flip the pages. A cathedral, Notre Dame, I think, in intricate detail. An old stone church. A modern skyscraper I don't recognize. A bridge that looks like it's made of a thousand strings. Too many beautiful things to count.

"You have talent," I say.

The book falls to the last page. On there it says, The Glossary of Happiness. There's a list of random words.

"What's this?" I ask.

He looks horrified, and holds his hand out for the book.

"Mr. T. gave me an article. You remember?"

I think back. I do remember. I meant to ask him.

"That's right. What was it about?"

"It is about, how you say . . . professors? Collecting words that only mean something in one language. Like in Finland they have a word, sisu. In English it would be like 'sticking to it,' but there's no real English word for this, or Greek, either. Or in German, there is a word, Heimat, which means where you feel you belong. The article . . . it stayed with me. What a beautiful thing to collect words, no? It made me think about how we all feel the same things, all over the world. So I started a notebook. Maybe I want to collect words too."

I smile. "What a great idea," I say.

He blushes. "Anyway . . . You. You are the one with talent. Mr. T. always talking about your poems. You sent yours to the competition already?"

Now it's my turn to feel uncomfortable. I shake my head. "No. Not yet."

"You are like . . . the girl with all the words. You learn English so fast. You should send in your poem. You do it?"

I nod. I could do it. Maybe I should do it.

"Good," he says, looking satisfied. Then he opens his notebook to a fresh page and begins to sketch. "Good," he says one more time, and I smile at my own notebook.

Good.

Neo's Glossary of Happiness

koselig: Norwegian, intimacy, warmth

cozy: άνετος

amata: Italian, loved

joy: Χαρά

moxie: courage

sonrisa: sunrise?

esperanza: hope

on the bright side: ☺

AN AFTERNOON LIKE FIRE CHAI

I imagined that Christmas would be a big deal in the US, from all the American movies I saw back home, but I wasn't prepared for just how *everywhere* it would be. The day after Thanksgiving, a fire truck ripped through town at low speed with sirens blaring. I ran to my window to figure out what was going on, and, instead of an emergency, I saw Santa Claus on top, throwing candy at little kids squealing on the sidewalk. That set the tone. By the time we got back to school on Monday, Christmas had assaulted every surface of the school.

Of course we did Christmas back home, but nothing like this. My parents always used to grumble that when they were little, Christmas was barely a thing at all, and they got their presents on el día de los Reyes. That's the sixth of January, the day on which, tradition says, the three kings brought baby Jesus their gifts of frankincense, myrrh, and gold. That had changed by the time I was little. We all got together on the twenty-fourth and, at midnight, would open some gifts after we were stuffed full of empanadas and asado.

But here it's like a decoration store threw up all over everything. A few kids have wrapped their lockers in red-and-green candy-cane wrapping paper. There is a tree by the office. There are other decorations I haven't seen before from other celebrations that also happen in December. But the true king seems to be Santa Claus, adorning classroom doors and a rollaway mural outside the gym. And it's not just in the school, either. On my way to school that Monday, I saw the garbage truck guys hanging giant stars from every light post. On the walk home that night, after a movie with Neo, every star was lit up, as if they were showing me the way home.

It's contagious, all this showy desire to celebrate.

Altagracia seems to have made a decision that her

outfit and makeup will be a different holiday theme each day. Today she's in what seems to be a nod to an elf costume, with tight brown corduroy pants, booties with flaps turned down, and all her hair piled on the top of her head and a little elf-hat hairpin in front of it. Her makeup is subtle, to let the outfit do the talking. I wonder how early she gets up every day to coordinate all this "fabulosity," as she would say.

She's giving me a rundown of her day. "So I got a great little sample bag from this indie organic makeup company—amazing, right?—and so I'm doing a sponsored post. ### ## #######. And . . ."

From the corner of my eye I see Harrison is sprinting, all legs and arms, in my direction. For a second I wonder if he's going to tackle someone behind me, so I turn around. But, no, he's aiming straight at me. He's . . .

He's hugging me. I freeze, same as if a flock of singing birds had just decided to circle me, animated-movie style. It feels that special, that unlikely.

"You're a genius! I'm actually going to show this test to my parents. This is awesome."

He shoves a crinkled paper in my face. I pull back a little to focus on the page. "Eighty-seven!" I smile.

"Solid B-plus territory. Which is, like, a serious

improvement." It's now that he notices Altagracia. "Oh, hey, Gracie. Sorry, were you guys in the middle of something? I was just so excited."

She waves an elegant burgundy-tipped hand at him. "Not at all, nerd-ball. I've got a video to shoot. I'll send you a link to a rough cut later, Ana," she says, flinging her bag over her shoulder.

"Okay, cool," I say.

I look back at Harrison as Altagracia walks away. He wears happy very well. That is a new expression I have learned. To wear an emotion like it is clothes. I love it.

"What are you doing right now?" he asks.

"I'm . . . just getting my stuff to go home."

"You like coffee?"

"Not so much."

"#####?"

"I like tea," I offer.

"Okay, tea, great. Let me hydrate you in thanks for how much you've helped me."

"Accepted," I say. I am proud to be able to use a word that Altagracia just taught me the other day.

"Awesome, come on. Green Man?"

"Sure." I say sure like, *whatever*. But I *feel* like *ohmygod*.

At the restaurant, we get a booth in front of the window. He slides in first, and there's just enough room for me when I get in. We're sitting so close together that I can feel the warmth of his leg on mine. Closer than in the library. It quickens my pulse.

He studies the menu, although I imagine he's seen it probably hundreds of times. Even I can remember the highlights.

"What are you having?" he asks finally.

The menu has things with wild names, like Cocoa-Demon and Archangel, different globs of ice cream with exotic sauces and creams.

"I'll have the fire chai. How about you?"

"I may need to up my game. I was going to have a vanilla latte. Want to share an Opprobrium?"

It's one of the ice cream mixes. I don't even look at the menu for which types. I just nod. He signals to the waitress and she takes our order.

The fire chai is fiery. It starts like regular tea, but then begins to burn on my tongue and on the inside of my cheeks, going finally to my lips. Harrison watches me drink it. "What's it like?" he asks. I want to lean my lips to his and give him a taste, but, gah, no. Of course not that. So I hand him the cup. He keeps his eyes steady on mine as he takes a sip.

He hands it back. "That is *hot*! So is the ########## true? You eat a lot of spice?"

I laugh. "We actually don't cook with a lot of spice at all. But fire chai . . . I wanted to know."

He's still keeping eye contact in a way he doesn't while we're studying. "So . . . was it what you'd hoped it would be?"

It seems to be a question about something other than tea. The heat from the chair is making my neck hot. Or maybe he is. I'm not sure how to answer, so I look at the table and say, "Yes."

Then out of the corner of my eye I catch some kids from school walking past. Harrison sees them too and waves.

The Opprobrium arrives. Two spoons, enough mint chocolate chip ice cream for a whole band, striped Hershey's kisses on top. I take a spoonful. For some reason I am transported to *Lady and the Tramp*, the scene where they're sharing a bowl of spaghetti. I want to eat without spoons until we both get to the bottom and . . .

Get ahold of yourself, Ana.

"Ana, do you have plans on New Year's?"

I swallow my tea, even though my throat already feels like it is on fire. Is he . . . asking me out?

I look at him. Too long, apparently.

"Sorry, of course, you have a thing. It's only in a few weeks. I . . . that was dumb . . ."

"No, no. I was just thinking. No, I don't think . . . I thought I had a thing but, no."

"They're doing live music here, actually. It's sort of ##### ##### . . . anyway, if you wanted to check it out."

I smile. Yes, this felt like a date. But plans for New Year's? That is something more, no? You don't ask just anyone out on a holiday. "Yes. I like that," I say.

"Good." He blows out a breath, almost like he was nervous, and I very nearly grab the sides of his face to kiss him. "Good." Then he picks up a cookie from the plate and swoops it along the ice cream. "These remind me of the cookies I used to put out for Santa."

"You put out cookies?"

"Sure. Don't you guys?"

We don't. Our tradition feels a lot harder to explain, so I decide to leave out the parts about the three kings and the hay and just tell him the part I think he'll understand.

"No. We have dinner on Christmas, open the presents at midnight."

"At midnight?" he says.

"Yes. When the twenty-fourth becomes the twenty-fifth."

"So technically the day before Christmas?"

I scrunch up my eyebrows. I run the conversation over in my head. Maybe I said something wrong. "Christmas. December twenty-fourth," I say.

He smiles, cocks his head. "Christmas is on the twenty-fifth."

"I mean . . ." What is the word? The twenty-fifth is the official day, sure, but not the day you celebrate. I don't know how to say all that.

He apparently has opinions about it too, because he launches into a big explanation. But it's a whole lot of #### ##### ######## ### ###### #### to me.

I never even imagined it would be different here. I say, "The twenty-fifth is like . . . the day after the wedding."

"Wait, what? You guys have weddings on Christmas?" asks Harrison, confused.

I shake my head and laugh. That was the wrong example, or maybe I said it wrong. "No," I say. "The twenty-fourth is everything. Dinner. Presents at midnight. The twenty-fifth is . . . the after."

"You mean . . . no running down first thing in the

morning for presents that magically appear under the tree?" He looks at me like he might cry.

"First thing in the morning? Why would anyone get up early on a holiday?" I ask. An honest question. It sounds awful.

He laughs, explaining how they do it. Apparently his parents make him *sleep* and then *wait until the next day* to open presents in some kind of child torture tradition.

"Wait, but they did that to you when you were little too?" I ask.

"Of course. Santa comes overnight."

I shake my head. Some things in America make sense. Some things are meatballs.

But some things are still bananas.

ONE LITTLE BOX
INSIDE ANOTHER

I like Mr. T.'s ideas for field trips, usually. But who thought strapping knives to the bottom of boots in order to screech around a sheet of ice was a good idea? I'd like to find the inventor of this concept and kick them. If only I could get off my butt.

I hate ice skating.

Mr. T. knows the manager of an ice rink that is close to the school. He somehow convinced the school to let us use one of the buses. He found us "free ice time" between hockey players and figure skaters. I imagine something like gratitude might be in order, but all I can muster is a simmering frustration.

Why can't I stand up?

It is not always warm back home. But we do not have enough icy surfaces for a thing like this near where I lived. I've watched ice skaters on television and, if I'm honest, imagined I might be good at this.

I am not good at this.

Neo goes by, scrunched like he's barreling down a mountain. Except he's moving a few centimeters, and screeching to a halt, then moving a foot awkwardly to get a little more propulsion. Mr. T. is as wobbly as the rest of us.

Neo circles back to me. "Need help?" he asks, holding out a hand. He doesn't appear to be in any position to offer help, but I take his hand. He holds mine firm. I get up on my skates. Slowly.

"You like this?" I ask once I'm standing up.

He shrugs. "Better than verb tenses." He smiles.

I admire his attitude about it. I screech my right skate forward. I used to love roller skating. Why is this not that? I screech my left skate forward. Neo stays next to me, smiling in encouragement.

"See? You get better," he lies. I appreciate the attempt.

I start gliding. Okay, no, gliding is too smooth a word for it. I start moving forward without falling. Neo skates a bit ahead of me. He tries to turn around to do it backward. *Oh, no, he's going down.* But he doesn't, at the last minute. I laugh. He lights up, the ice making his eyes even brighter, it seems.

Mr. T. takes a massive spill. He was going fast, apparently about to do some kind of jump, and wipes out spectacularly against the side.

Neo and I make our way to him.

"Having fun?" He smiles ruefully, rubbing his knee.

"Are you okay?" I ask.

He nods slowly, but he looks sad. "You like ice skating?" he asks, looking at me hopefully.

My heart squeezes a little. It's weird to think of teachers as humans, as people who care if other people think they're doing a good job.

"I don't." I smile. My mother would say that the kind thing would be to lie. But I want to cheer him up with the truth.

He laughs, and Neo does too.

"You know why I brought you here?" he asks. "My dad was real into hockey when I was a kid. My brothers too. But no matter how much I tried to get the hang of it, I just never did. No sense of balance, I guess.

And ##### ######### ##### I try to imag-
ine what it must be like for you guys, learning a new
language, #######, moving from a new place . . .
just trying to get your balance . . . well, ######
####### skating, and how I was, y'know, always
on my butt. I thought maybe it could be fun, being on
our butts together."

"I understand," I say. Mr. T. tries very hard.

"Me too," says Neo.

"Go get off the ice, you two. You look truly miserable out there." He laughs. "Go get a soda or something,"
he says, waving his hand in the direction of the little
café at the front of the rink.

Neo has his skates off so fast I wonder if they were
even laced. I take mine off too and find my shoes. We
make our way to the café.

"The year is almost finished, right?" he asks halt-
ingly. "What do you do for . . . during vacation?" He
looks red. I wonder if he's still cold, even though it's
toasty in the café.

"I don't know. Christmas with my family." I keep
out the part about my New Year's plans with Harrison,
although I don't exactly know why. "You?"

He studies his soda can intently. "Yeah, Christmas.
We're going . . . lots to do." He smiles.

But it's a sad smile, not lighting up his eyes the way his real smiles do. I wonder if he's thinking of home, about what the first holidays away will be like, like I am.

"You miss home sometimes?" I ask. I've asked him before, but I've learned that missing home is a little box you keep unwrapping only to find another one inside. That missing home isn't an event that ends, but colored glasses you wear always.

He looks up at me, and I am struck all over again by his blue eyes. They are almost translucent blue, with flecks of gold you'd miss if you didn't really look. "I want to be . . . happy," he says.

It's not quite an answer, but I think I get what he means by it. "Me too," I agree.

I want to be happy, too.

NOCHE DE PAZ

Our tiny living room looks beautiful. Festive. Our tree is a little scraggly, and the decorations all came out of one giant tube from the discount store, but it brightens the cramped corner where we put it. And while there's not a lot of money for piles of presents, there are enough boxes under the tree to set that little flutter alive in me. When I was little, my father used to have to put a napkin over the clock because I wouldn't eat waiting for midnight, when we could open the presents.

My dad has put on Christmas carols. As one of my favorites plays in English, the old way echoes in my head. "Silent night" doesn't quite mean "Noche de paz." I wonder why they chose "silence" instead of "peace" for the English version. Is silence peace to some people?

Because, as someone who has often been silent these last few months, I've noticed it can be one of the least peaceful things.

But tonight? Tonight the quiet is peace.

The first Christmas with my father in almost four years

Homemade eggnog and empanadas and presents for a
girl
that existed four years ago,
the one who still liked monkeys on zippered bags for
her pencils.
But it is also the warm smell of him hugging me,
his aftershave strong, his chin rough,
and my mother smiling, her eyes glassy with barely
held-in happy tears.

WHEN ESCAPE IS REQUIRED, CHECK THE KITCHEN

Altagracia and I pull up to Green Man on New Year's Eve. She is driving and talking fast, like she's excited on my behalf. "Okay, so this is a known New Year's thing to do, which is a good sign. ###### ###### ########. Not that he's like that," she says, glancing in my direction nervously. "Also, there's a certain significance to the night, which means it's not just a whatever thing, you know? And there's the obligatory midnight kiss, so it can be all like, 'Oh, it's just New Year's, whatever,' ######## ####### #### #######. So overall a good choice."

When I mentioned that Harrison had asked me

out for New Year's Eve, Altagracia insisted that she do my makeup. She picked out an outfit for me from her closet, a simple black dress that squeezes me in all the right places. She also flat-ironed my hair pin straight, and made my eyes look like twice their normal size. My parents think I'm sleeping over at her house tonight, which, actually, I do intend to do. She and her family will be going to a big party and staying at a hotel tonight, so she gave me the code to her back door. Otherwise I would not have been allowed out past midnight, New Year's Eve or no.

"You look like a rock star. Truly. ##### ######## stunning. His pasty ass is going to wonder what on earth he did to get lucky enough for you to go on a date with him." She beams at me, middle schooler mixed with proud mama. "Now shoo. Out you go. I've got to go deal with my father's extremely boring dentist friends and their hundred-year-old wives. Lucky me." She complains about her dad sometimes, but she secretly seems to be looking out for him. She could have gone out on New Year's with anyone from school, but although she pretends to be annoyed to be going to a formal party with her dad, it's obviously what she chose. She's funny that way, a soft heart under a hard shell.

She kisses me on the cheek—a real kiss, not an air kiss. I am grateful we've become friends, although I'm not always 100 percent sure why she wanted to. I am nowhere near as cool as she is.

"Thank you so much," is all I say.

I step out. The air has taken an unexpected turn in the last week to the iciest dagger air I've ever felt in my life. I'm not dressed for it. The black pantyhose are barely a layer; my jacket is nothing more than a black satin cowl-neck belted thing Altagracia put over the dress for effect at the last minute. The wind whips through me. *Don't die of hypothermia on your way to the door.*

I'm so wrapped up in the cold and the awkwardness of this moment that it takes me a bit to look toward the Green Man entrance. Where will he be? What if he's not here yet?

A figure is jumping up and down in the cold, waving her hand like she's calling in an airplane. Frankie. She and Britt are wearing jeans and puffy jackets. Britt is in a woolen hat threatening to eat her head. Ugh. Again I wore the wrong thing. I feel like I've worn a wedding gown for a trip to a coffee shop. But it's New Year's. How are they not dressed up for New Year's?

"Hey!" she says. "You made it! Happy almost next year! Let's get inside. It's cold as balls out here."

Balls are cold? "Sure," I say.

Frankie opens the door. A wall of sound hits. They've cleared all but the bar-height tables, and they've set up a tiny makeshift bandstand in the corner. A band is screeching out some very noisy rock-funk-rap mash-up. No one is dancing, because it's not exactly dancing music.

Frankie pulls me toward a corner. "Here, let's put our stuff down."

I follow her. "Have you seen Harrison?" I ask over the music.

"What?" yells Frankie back at me.

"Harrison!" I yell louder.

"Oh, he's over there somewhere." She waves to the dance floor behind me. I turn to see what she's looking at.

Harrison. So handsome in a button-down that's not tucked into his jeans, hair more combed than usual, color high on his cheeks. He's holding something that's shaped like a beer bottle, although this place is dry. His lips look perfect, and he's cleanly shaven in a way that makes my heart hold still a second.

Apparently it has the same effect on Jessica, who is standing just an inch in front of him, blond hair tipped back, eyes straight on him. I know that look. That "you've got all my attention" tractor-beam look you give a guy when you're hoping he'll kiss you.

She puts her hand on his shoulder. It's casual, but it's not.

She's smiling at him and I know that smile, because it is the smile I give Harrison too.

Britt leans over to Frankie. "If I didn't know better, I'd say *that's* not over."

I run that statement through a thousand calculations a minute. Is she talking about . . . I follow where she's looking. Yes, she's definitely looking at Harrison and Jessica. Not over . . . *like they used to go out? Do go out?* I stare at them stupidly. Every moment I've ever caught her looking at us flashes through my mind in a sickening trailer. The sharp stares in math class while Harrison and I talked. Her icy reception of me at the lunch table. Of course. How have I missed it until this moment? "They used to go out?" I ask. I try to keep my tone casual, to not look too pathetic, but I'm not sure I succeed.

Frankie's shoulders fall. "Oh my God, did you not know?" She tugs at my elbow gently as she puts her stuff down on a tall chair, puffy jacket, bag. She's in a cute crop top with a baby–New Year cartoon figure on it.

Britt adds, "They were totally high-school-married. And then . . . Jess was stupid. She started dating this college guy. Harrison was a mess for a long time."

"It's nice to see they can be friends now," Frankie says pointedly, giving Britt a look. I turn around to glance at them again. Jessica's lips are curled into a heart. She does not seem like a friend.

She pushes onto the tiptoes of her high-tops. The lean in is slow, so slow. My throat tightens. The music fades back, it all turns hazy as my stomach gives a lurch. Her lips land on his. He stands there. I can't tell if he's shocked or happy or if he was the one to ask her to kiss him. She gets off her tippy toes and runs her thumb gently over his lips.

I want to throw up. I have been so wrong. So stupidly, densely, completely wrong.

My throat grows a hedgehog on the inside and it travels down, spiny side out, all the way down to my stomach, then the pit of my gut. *I. Am. So. Stupid. SO stupid.* I replay every conversation I've ever had with him, every time I thought he was flirting but clearly wasn't, every time I mooned over his eyelashes like an idiot. The stupidity is screaming in my ears. Or maybe he *was* flirting and he's just one of those guys.

I need to get out of here.

I need to get out. I want out *now*.

I turn to Frankie and Britt. Frankie is studying my face. Britt is talking to a waitress who is asking for our order and taking Britt's credit card.

"Hey, that was . . . ," Frankie begins. I put my hand to my ear in an "I can't hear you" gesture.

"I need to go to the bathroom," I lie. I don't have to, but I can't keep a calm face for much longer. I want to cry, or scream, or anything besides stand here with this seething hurt and frustration and huge sense of "I am an idiot." Somehow it feels like a concentrated version of how I walk around every day: missing cues, missing words, confused. Or maybe that's how dating is here. I don't even know. All I know is that I thought this boy liked me. But I was wrong.

"I'll come with you," says Frankie. But Britt leans in to ask her what she wants to order. The waitress looks impatient, like the order is taking too long. Frankie gets distracted.

"It's okay," I say, pulling away before she can follow.

I push into the crowd and head to where the bathrooms must be, near the back. But how am I going to get out through there?

It hits me: the kitchen. I once saw a video by a guy who used to be a spy, about how to survive in any situation. He said that when something bad happens in a restaurant, an explosion, or a terrorist attack, the mistake most people make is that they assume that the way they came in is the only way to get out. But it isn't. The best way to get out is the kitchen. This isn't a terrorist attack, but it feels a little like an explosion in my chest.

The kitchen.

I push in through the double doors. Instantly I'm in an entirely different world. Where outside it's all dark-gray walls and dark everything, here it is crisp white tile and bright lights. There's a guy at a grill, and another by a giant, rumbling machine.

The men in the kitchen are speaking Spanish. "Ayúdeme a llegar a la calle, por favor!" I say to him. "Tengo que irme." I have to go. This softens him.

"Venga por aquí, m'hijita," says the guy by the big machine. He leads me out the kitchen door, to an alley behind the restaurant. I nearly hug him.

He asks if my father is coming to pick me up. I tell him not to worry. But I can't imagine calling my father, with the multitude of lies I'd have to admit to him. The wind bites at my legs. I make my way to the alley and out to the side street, out of sight of anyone at the front of Green Man.

I open my recent texts. Altagracia. I can't bother her while she's at her party. She's done way too much for me already. My mom. My dad. *Nope.*

What am I going to do?

I skim past the nauseating final text from Harrison. *See you then!* All exclamation-point-y. I had let myself read that as such a tone of enthusiasm. Like he was as excited to see me as I was to see him.

Neo. I click on our most recent conversation. There's a Merry Christmas text. Then, before that, us debating whether to add nineties movies to Mr. T.'s list.

Neo. I could call Neo.

The wind whips up, sending ice into my sleeves, down my neck. I can't feel my fingers. Texting feels like trying to move blocks of wood at the ends of my hands.

Are u there? I ask.

The response comes back right away. *Yes. Happy New Year.*

I take a deep breath. This is so colossally stupid. But when it comes right down to it, I just can't think of who else I'd rather tell this to.

Neo, I need help. Can you pick me up?

Luckily he doesn't wait for me to say more. *I will be there right away.*

I share my location with him so he can see where to go.

The wind thrashes down from the river, slicing chills into my ankles, my fingers, my core. I will never go out without a full snowsuit ever again, even on New Year's.

And, because this night can't get any colder, a light snow begins to fall.

I jump up and down as I wait. The snowflakes really are flakes, delicate, lacy, rapaciously cold. I have never been in snowfall before. I want to relish the magic of it—it does look like magic—but I would like it a little better if I could feel my face.

I look up and down the road, watching for oncoming lights. Finally, a thin whine appears in the distance. I squint at it. But, no, it's some person on a scooter, the kind that I've seen delivery guys drive, the kind in old European movies. Who would ride such a thing in this weather?

The scooter draws closer, its whine turning into a

more full-throated hum. It's green, with a big purple patch on its side. It reaches the corner. I focus on the driver's face. It's Neo.

Neo on a green-and-purple scooter.

He stops in front of me. I stand still, a girl in a tiny black dress with snow swirling around me. I must look ridiculous.

"You look cold," he says, taking off his jacket, dusting the snow off me and wrapping it around my shoulders. His jacket is warm from his body.

"No, you'll freeze," I say. He's in just a long-sleeved T-shirt underneath.

"It's okay. My place is not far." He smiles and motions to his scooter, takes a mock bow. "My dragon."

I laugh and I climb on behind him as elegantly as I can, which is to say: not very. My legs and hands are still frozen, but my middle thaws out under his thick, warm jacket.

"Hold on," he says, and I lean into his warm, wiry back. Relief comes over me. I close my eyes and try to forget the reel of Jessica leaning up to kiss Harrison that spools over and over in my brain.

"Efgaristo," I say as the wind hits my face. *Thank you.* It's the one word of Greek he's taught me.

WELCOME TO MY PALACE

Neo lives just a couple of blocks from the school, over a shop with a cluttered window full of vacuum parts and half-disassembled televisions. It is on an industrial strip I've driven by before, but which I didn't realize had any apartments. A train track runs behind it. I wonder how loud it is when a train rumbles through.

We make our way up a set of stairs that list decidedly to the left, covered in what must have once been brown carpet but looks more now like old felt.

"You've seen my dragon, now welcome to my palace," he says as he opens the door. It may be a little sexist to say, but it looks like a place without women.

Nothing on the walls. An old green couch, a television on milk crates. A lamp with a bare bulb. Our house is humble, but my mother has brought fancy hand towels from home. She has hung pictures of us from our old lives. Our place looks like a family lives there. This place looks like no one in particular lives here.

But only one thing actually matters about Neo's place: it is warm.

"My father is working," he says.

I realize now why Neo had asked what I was doing during the holidays. Maybe that's why he seemed sad when we talked about it. I wonder how he felt all alone here on New Year's. "I've never seen your scooter before," I say instead.

"I just got it. Off Craigslist. A guy was moving and sold it for nothing. The engine is good. Needs a paint job."

It would be rude to agree, so I don't say anything.

We sit down on the couch. "So what happened?"

I explain. What I thought tonight was. What it actually was. Neo listens quietly. He seems to tense when I mention Harrison.

"I am sorry, Ana," he says.

I am finally warm enough to take off his jacket. I

hand it to him and thank him. It's warm enough that I also take off Altagracia's for-show black belted jacket.

I realize how tight my dress is now. "Do you have a . . . comfy shirt?" Embarrassment crawls up my neck. He's never seen me dressed anything like this. He goes in the next room and gets me a big beige T-shirt with an old-timey brown truck on it. Then he says, "How about a Greek movie? With English subtitles. You learn a little about my language tonight." He smiles. "Then maybe we find one in Spanish."

I smile. "Sure." He flicks on the TV, and it's tuned to the Greek channel already. On the screen, people are around an azure infinity-edge swimming pool, a glistening sea beyond, a yacht moored within view. A woman with beautiful black hair and an asymmetric blindingly white bathing suit is saying something to a man in a pink button-down, who holds a thick-bottomed glass half full of amber liquid. Neo hasn't turned on the subtitles yet, so I don't know what they're saying, although I want to laugh at how different the scene on the TV is from this frozen night in Neo's modest apartment.

Neo turns to me, his eyes earnest, the tips of his ears still red from the cold outside. "You look very pretty," he says. As if he'd been wondering what the right thing to say was since I took off the jacket.

"Thank you," I say and he turns back to the TV, the reflection of the blue pool lighting up his blue, blue eyes.

My heart flutters a little, and I look for something to say. "I found you a word," I blurt out. "For your list. The Glossary of Happiness."

If he's surprised, he doesn't show it. "What is the word?" he asks.

"Tarab," I say. "It's Arabic. A happiness that comes from music."

He smiles. "I like that." He pauses the movie and jots it down in the notes in his phone. Then he turns to the TV. "You see what is happening?" He gestures at the screen.

"Not even a little bit," I confess.

"He loves this woman, but he cannot tell her. You see? Her father is big boss. He is just worker. It is very sad."

I study him. He seems to be talking about more than the movie.

"Have you loved?" he asks. "A boy back home?"

I smile. "My parents don't like me dating," I say. "They never let me, at home. And here . . ." I trail off.

I think back. One boy I kissed at an outdoor dance near las viñas. Another one I met at an amusement park and he insisted on buying me a giant stuffed animal. Where did that go? Left behind with all my other things. I've liked boys, for sure. But love? No. He must know how I feel about Harrison, but I feel stupid saying it, especially after what happened tonight.

"It seems easier in the movies," he says.

I smile. I motion with my chin that he should put the movie back on. "Does he finally tell her? Do they get together?" I ask.

"Watch!" he says, laughing. We settle into the couch as the beautiful beach vistas play on the screen.

The apartment is warm, the T-shirt soft over my dress. That, and the comedown from all the tension and the cold, makes me as sleepy as I remember ever feeling. Neo is warm next to me. It makes me want to shift closer to him.

I don't know when I doze off, but all of a sudden I feel my head on his shoulder. It startles me awake. I look up at Neo, ready to apologize, but he is looking at me, a small smile on his lips.

"It is the New Year," he tells me. "I didn't want you to miss it."

I turn to the TV. He's put on the channel with the

celebration from New York. Two men, one with white hair, laugh and jump up and down. The camera shots change. The ball shines. The number of the new year flashes. Neo turns up the sound. A song starts to play. The camera pans the crowd.

He sits up. "We dance?"

I laugh and stand up. He stands up too. It's awkward. I'm not sure what kind of dance he means. He puts his arm around my waist gingerly. He takes my other hand in his, the old-fashioned way of dancing. I step in closer and we sway slowly. The music is a little sad, about people you've lost or things you've forgotten, but it's being played in a loud and festive way. On the screen, couples kiss.

I look up at Neo. He's so close, a few inches away. He looks at me steadily, his eyes on my face. "Happy New Year," he whispers. I feel myself pulled in. His lips look perfect, the dimple in his chin a little shadowed where he missed a spot shaving. I run my eyes over his face. I've never been this close to him.

The air suspends, everything slows down. The din from the television fades. It is a new year. I am in a place I didn't expect to be, looking at someone I didn't expect to be looking at. Maybe life is like this, the moments that come, not the ones we try to make.

My phone clangs. My text tone. Is it always that loud? I look down. On my lock screen, there it is. Harrison's name. There's a happy new year wish from Valentina too. I scrunch down to look closer.

Hey, where'd u go? Happy New Year! I wish you were her.

Is that a typo? Or a confession? I scrunch down to look closer.

Neo takes a step back. "I'll let you get that. Sprite?" he asks. He walks to the kitchen. The moment, whatever the moment was, is gone.

QUÉ VERGÜENZA

It is my first day back from vacation, and I am actually dreading math class. I haven't seen Harrison since the mess on New Year's. He texted me, all those times that night, a few times the next day, another yesterday. I ignored the texts because I didn't know what to say. To the one yesterday, the *what happened?* I figured I'd have to say something because I'd be seeing him in school today. I answered, *sorry, something came up.* I don't want to explain any of it, how I misunderstood everything. How I felt at seeing him with Jessica. How everything that night was like believing I could speak English only to learn I understood nothing at all.

I keep thinking about Neo, too, and our almost-kiss. Was it an almost-kiss? It felt that way, but maybe I misunderstood. And if it was an almost-kiss, did I want it to be an actual-kiss?

Harrison slips into his seat. I look down at my notes intently, like I'm studying. Embarrassment crawls up my neck with prickly feet.

"Hey," he says to me. The teacher isn't here yet, and there's a low hum in the room.

"Hey," I say.

"You okay? ####### understand what happened." His eyes look genuinely worried. The kind of look I might have taken for some other kind of interest, before.

"Oh, yeah." I wave my hand breezily, like I am often in the habit of midparty kitchen escapes. "Something came up. Had to go."

"Sure, yeah . . ." He looks down at his hands and then glances back at me. "Well, I was wondering if you'd be around on Thursday after school, to study? Quiz on Friday."

I look at him. He is still so handsome in a burgundy hoodie and unshaved fuzz on his jaw. For my own sake, I should stay away from him. Also, if he's with Jessica, that is their business. And, more than anything, I am tired of thinking I understand this new language, this new world, only to discover I am a foreigner all over again.

"I can't," I say.

"Oh. You want to do Wednesday instead?" he asks.

I shake my head. I once thought it would be bananas to spend time with Harrison. Now I realize it was bananas.

All I know is I can't let myself do it again. "Sorry," I say, and turn back to my book.

HAY FOR THE CAMELS

Los Reyes is strange this year. It's a holiday, but no one seems to know it is. I guess I understood this but wasn't completely prepared for it. School is open. Everyone is walking around. It pulls at me that no one knows that half a world away, it is one of the most important days of the year.

I don't stay for a movie or to tutor Harrison. My dad doesn't pick me up, which he does some days. Although I don't usually mind the walk, that oversight stings today too. Maybe he's forgotten as well.

The apartment is still when I open the door. For a moment I wonder if my mom is out shopping. When she's home there's the sound of her voice talking to people back home, almost always, or wooden spoons clanging inside pots. But today there's none of that. She's sitting in the kitchen, quietly looking at the window, as if the window didn't give only a view of a wall.

"Hola, mi niña," she says.

"Pasa algo?" I ask. It is both strange and liberating that she's not even giving a nod to the English-only rule.

"I couldn't find hay," she says. And she puts her face in her hands and cries.

Hay. For the three kings' camels. On Three Kings, we always put a little bit of hay and a bowl of water out for the camels. I stopped believing in that years ago, of course, but somehow we kept doing it. At first I was annoyed. I thought the fact that my mom wanted to keep doing it meant she thought I was still a baby who believed the three kings were really coming. But, eventually, I came to like the ritual of it. Somewhere, thousands of years and even more thousands of miles away, there had been camels, and putting out a little bit of hay was an acknowledgment to the tradition the men on those camels started. She always made the hay and water disappear by the next morning, filling me with the feeling of *maybe.* Maybe it's okay to believe, even when you don't. I know camels and kings aren't coming, but I want to live in a world that celebrates they do.

"Ma," I say, "Don't cry."

"I went to the store. None of them had it, like at home. I tried to ask, but I . . ."

"Ma, come on. Don't be sad. I have an idea."

She comes meekly, which makes me even sadder. I arm myself with her kitchen shears and walk her down to the little courtyard outside our building. The grass has long since dried out.

"In the United States, the camels have learned to eat dry grass."

Her face is still splotchy from crying, but she smiles through it and nods. I crouch down and cut a few handfuls. We take it up to the apartment and put it on a plate, along with a bowl of water, near the window that won't open because it's painted shut and which no one wants to open much because it faces a wall. But still, she smiles.

The next morning, the grass and the water are gone.

Reyes Magos,

Ha pasado mucho tiempo y estoy a muchos kilómetros de distancia. Do you speak English? I'm trying. If you're a magic king, you must speak English, no? At least as much as Spanish.

I'm sorry I stopped believing in you. I thought it was part of growing up. But in this place, I need you. We need you. I think my mother needs you even more than I do.

Holding on to you feels important. The stories we tell ourselves make us who we are, and you are who I am. I close my eyes and see you crossing the long distances, far away from home, looking for the truth lit only by a faraway star. I understand you. There will always be a place for you with us. I will always leave hay and water for your camels. Don't forget me.

THE ELEPHANT IN THE ROOM

Altagracia runs up to me squealing and grabs me by the wrists and jumps in front of my locker. A few kids turn around with quizzical looks, but she doesn't seem to care.

"What?" I ask, jumping with her. Her enthusiasm is contagious.

She lands and crouches a little, as if preparing to be tackled. "You just can't, under any circumstances, guess the goodness of this day."

"You got a good grade in chemistry?" I ask.

She throws her hands up. "Bigger! Much bigger."

"New car? Cool vacation?"

"No, no. What's like the thing I want more than anything?" She is positively vibrating with the news.

"Beyoncé reposted one of your videos?"

She shakes her head. "Okay, the second most?"

"Sponsorship?"

"Sponsorship!!!" she squeals in a pitch close to one only dogs can hear.

"Congratulations! Tell me everything."

So she does. But she insists on doing it while we do something called aerial yoga. She has signed us up for some type of torture involving fabric ribbons attached to the ceiling. She drives us there after school giving me the blow-by-blow of how the sponsorship happened.

We pull up to the studio, a little storefront in the next town over. It's got purple fabric draped in the windows and a blue stone statue with a rhinestone necklace on it sitting on luxurious reams of orange fabric. As we step inside, the door makes a gentle tinkling sound, like a crystal bell.

"This place is so cool," I tell her.

"My dad's new girlfriend owns the studio," she whispers.

The woman running the class is long and muscular. She leads us through a series of stretches, using the fabric ribbons hanging from the ceiling. She makes it look like she's floating and the ribbons just artfully twirl themselves around her. Altagracia and I are far less graceful but she gives us time to get the hang of it.

I wrap the ribbon around my hips, the way I just learned how to do, and hang upside down to let the blood rush to my head. Altagracia does the same, facing me. It reminds me of hanging my head upside down from the couch when I was little.

"So we going to talk about the elephant in the room?" says Altagracia.

I look around. I know she can't mean an actual elephant, but . . . ?

She smiles. Her face is getting red from hanging upside down. Mine must be too. "It means 'the big thing that's obvious but we're trying to pretend isn't here.'"

"The elephant in the room," I repeat. I love these unexpected gifts in English, these delightful little bundles of creativity that sneak up on me when I least expect it. "I like that. So what's this elephant?"

"New Year's. What happened with Harrison? You're going to have to talk about it at some point."

"It was stupid," I say. "I was a head up my ass." I try one of the expressions I've learned these last months.

"That's not quite how that saying goes, but okay. Say more."

"It was never a date. I got that wrong. He is with Jessica."

Altagracia tips her head to the side. "Is he? I hadn't heard that was back on."

"You knew?"

"I mean, yeah, but that was like ancient history. Jessica was kind of a dog to him. I'd like to think he's smarter than that."

I close my eyes, picturing the way she leaned toward him, like it was the most natural thing in the world.

"I didn't even stay for midnight. I went to Neo. From ESL. We watched a Greek movie."

I want to tell her about my head on Neo's shoulder, the held-breath moment during the dance before my phone dinged and the moment was broken. But I don't know what it means, let alone how to explain it. I flip back right side up. My head is hot and woozy. I take a deep breath and close my eyes. Little explosions of light behind my eyelids are like a field of stars.

"That's interesting," she says, but doesn't add more, although she seems like there's something else on her mind.

"I feel so stupid," I say.

"You are not stupid." Altagracia flips right-side up too. "You put yourself out there, and that's great."

"I don't know," I say.

"It is," she says. "Have I told you about when I first got here? This reminds me of that feeling, the feeling I think you're trying to explain, of how maybe you're just never going to understand all the ins and outs of these people."

I nod. "Like I'm missing things all the time."

She moves her head in agreement. "So when I first came here, it was rough for me. I was different, and people don't always like different. And I knew enough to, like . . . be me. But maybe it wasn't the whole me, does that make any sense? It was one of the things that made me want to get to know you that first day. There aren't a lot of us Spanish speakers here. And not that that's everything. I know our lives are different in a lot of ways. But the way you came here and are trying to make your life here. You just put yourself out there. The whole you." She looks away, like she's remembering, or maybe trying not to. "I guess what I'm saying is I've always been Gracie here. No one could say my name. So I gave myself a new one. I watched what they cared about, and that's what I showed about myself. Little by little I built that up. Gracie with the cool house. Gracie with the fine nails. Gracie with all the Instagram followers. The truth is, everyone wants to be friends with *Gracie*, not me. You could say that when you got here I was in the middle of a thing. Some people had been shitty to me last year, and I'm reevaluating everything. That's why I've sort of pulled back from the social scene at school. Like, I want to see things from a different angle, not just get caught up in this small-town stuff."

I shake my head, not fully understanding. "You are the most unique person I know, Altagracia. And you put yourself out there for so many people to see."

"Yeah, but it's not all of me. Even if I *am* all that." She laughs, and then looks at me, serious. "Do you know I've never even had a girlfriend?"

"Really?" I ask. We never actually talked about it, but I always assumed Altagracia had lots of girlfriends. "But you're so . . ."

"Confident? Outgoing?" Altagracia smiles. "I know it seems that way. But it's different to be all this"—she motions to her fabulous self—"than to be . . . like . . . actually open. Like, vulnerable." She laughs, embarrassed. "It's hard opening yourself up like that. Social media is one thing, that's just my brand. But you . . . You put your *heart* out there. I wish I were more like you."

I smile and grab her hand.

"There must be someone you like," I say.

She makes a face. An "I've got a secret" face.

"There is!" I squeaky-voice.

"It's . . . I mean, who knows."

"Who?"

She takes in a deep breath. "You know Leticia? From art?"

I go through my memory banks. I do know her. She's tall, with perfect posture, has a bunch of cartilage piercings and a laugh that comes straight from her belly. No matter what the assignment is, she always gives her piece great graphic-art flare. "Yeah," I say.

"Well, we were working on a project in my government class, and she's so smart and fearless. Like really up on politics in a way that's almost intimidating. Plus she's got this long, graceful neck."

I laugh. "Neck?"

"Don't judge. We've all got our things."

"You should totally go for it. Ask her out," I say.

She puffs out her cheeks, lets out the air. "We'll see."

"She'd be lucky to have you in her life."

She blushes. "You're something else, you know that?"

I smile at her. "You have a beautiful heart, Altagracia."

She cocks her head to one side, then waves her hand, like pushing away a fly, a thing you want to go away. "Anyway, back to you. What I'm trying to say is: It's Harrison's loss. You deserve someone who's crazy about you."

"Crazy . . . ?"

"Really into you!" She smiles. "Crazy in love. Like Beyoncé."

"It is always like Beyoncé, is it not?" I say.

She looks at me gravely. "It is."

We both laugh.

ESL CLASS, MEDIUM RARE

My heart does a little dance when I walk into ESL class and the desks are all jumbled up. Something new! I always like Mr. T.'s creative classes best.

"You're here!" he says. He is in a tuxedo T-shirt and an actual red bow tie. "Come on, come on, let's get started." We all crowd in for him to explain. He's set up a series of "regular" situations we may face out in the world. A few have props. The doctor's office, for example, has a stethoscope and a white lab coat. The mechanic's garage has a big cutout of a car. There's an airport check-in counter (just a podium with a hand-drawn TSA seal) and a big foam board with a well-drawn set of bookshelves on it, with a sign that says Librarian in front of it. And two desks are put together, draped in a red checkered tablecloth with a plate in front of each seat. A restaurant.

He explains. We'll each draw a partner and a station from two jars he's holding. For about ten minutes, we'll do our best to carry on a conversation that would be likely to happen in each of these places. We can make up whatever it is. There are words written on index cards at each station. In ten minutes, we'll pick new partners and new stations.

I'm partnered with Soo. I do my best to explain my imaginary aches while she fidgets in her white lab coat. When I tell her my belly hurts and she cocks her head quizzically and points to my head as if asking a question, I burst out laughing, and she does too.

When the timer rings, Soo leans over to me conspiratorially and says, "Belly is ugly word in English. Like noise that comes out when swallow air with food."

I laugh out loud. "Yes," I say.

My last partner of the period is Neo. We sit at the "restaurant table." Mr. T. has been playing waiter to each duo who had a turn at this station.

There are actual menus on top of the plates. I don't

understand all of it. One of the items is "pork belly." I laugh to myself, wanting to show Soo when the bell rings.

"And what can I get you started with?" asks Mr. T. with a white napkin draped over his bent forearm. The instructions say to pick an appetizer first.

Neo begins, "Started with . . . Mr. T., is cheese really blue? Is spelled wrong."

Mr. T. smiles. "Bleu cheese. It's got some indeterminate color banded in there, but, no, it is not all blue. Like a whitish creamy color mostly."

Neo nods. "Good then. Bleu cheese tater tots."

"I like the sliders." The description makes them sound like miniature hamburgers, although I'm not sure why they slide, but they sound delicious.

"You guys are naturals," says Mr. T., pretending to write it all down. "I'll be right back with those appetizers."

There are no appetizers, of course. He just goes over to help the other groups. But Neo is fully in character, so he keeps studying the menu. He also looks over the words we need to work into the conversation: *Can I get a refill?* One index card has a list to choose from: *rare, medium, well.*

"What are you having for dinner?" he asks me, a twinkle lighting up his face.

"I think steak," I say. I am already learning that my family and I like steak more than most people here, it seems. A dinner without steak was often thought to be a lesser meal, back home. But here a lot of people eat just vegetables.

"I like fish," Neo says. I'm not sure I recognize all the words in the fish section.

He begins to pretend to eat something. "Would you like some bread?" he offers.

Mr. T. comes over with our invisible appetizers. "Your tater tots and your sliders," he says.

Neo pantomimes picking up the plate and dumping them all in his mouth at once. He thrusts the imaginary platter at Mr. T. "Can I get a refill?" he asks.

Mr. T. laughs out loud. "FYI, that's usually for drinks, but well played, sir. A man after my own heart. And what can I get you for your main course?"

Neo is in full swing, with a goofy, playful air I never see in him. "Sir, what fish you recommend?"

"Well, the halibut is very fresh and prepared beautifully today," Mr. T. says, puffing up like a proud papa at how game Neo is.

"I take that. My girlfriend likes steak," he says. His eyes sparkle.

Girlfriend hangs in the air. I know he means girl and friend, but even so, the phrase sends a little shiver through me.

Mr. T. turns to me, "How would you like that cooked?"

"Medium is not too burned?" I ask.

He nods.

"Okay, medium."

Mr. T. pretends to write it all down and walks away.

"If this was a real restaurant, we would do . . . I don't know the English word. In Spanish it's sobremesa."

"What's that?" he asks.

"It means . . . well, the exact definition is like 'over table.' I haven't found a word in English for it. It means the time you spend after a meal, just talking, with the hours passing by and you don't even notice them. It's the best part of the dinner."

"Sobremesa," he says. "I like that." His Spanish pronunciation is surprisingly good. Neo smiles at me. "I think I would like American restaurant," he says.

What does he mean, I wonder. That he's never been to one here? I've only been because of Altagracia, and once at Green Man with Harrison, although that's more of a café. I imagine for a second going on a date with Neo. It's not hard to picture, actually. It would be comfortable, like all those hours spent laughing and puzzling over movies.

His face says more, but if he's thinking other things, he doesn't say them. When our meal is over, he pretends to grab the check. He pulls back my chair for me and I give him a little hug in thanks.

"That was fun," he says with a smile. "We do it again sometime."

I smile back. "I would like that."

NOT ON THE SAME PAGE

I forgot my lunch today. I briefly toy with the idea of just skipping lunch altogether, but my stomach is rumbling.

I walk into the cafeteria and get on the line. I'm keeping my gaze down, trained on the sandwiches, when I feel a tap on my shoulder.

I look back. "Frankie," I say.

"I was beginning to worry that aliens had ######## you."

I miss part of that, and I just shake my head no.

"Why don't you sit with us at lunch anymore?"

I haven't sat with Harrison, Britt, Frankie, and

Jess since the debacle at New Year's. Because I've been bringing lunch from home, it's been easy to just avoid them. Harrison said something after the first day, but now he is just awkward around me, not saying anything at all.

But how do I explain all that? A creeping heat prickles my neck, my ears. The words are swimming out of reach all of a sudden.

She pulls up next to me. "What happened on New Year's?"

"I had to go," I say, finally finding something to say.

"It was Harrison and Jess, wasn't it?"

The line has moved in front of the sandwiches. I grab a foil-wrapped one.

"I have to . . ." I don't know what I have to do. I walk up to the cashier and pay her in quarters. I had to scrape the bottom of my schoolbag for enough for lunch. Now Frankie is watching me and I don't know if this could get any more humiliating.

Then I head to the door. She follows. She blocks my path, but gently.

"Hey, talk to me for a second. Okay? We don't have to stay here. I'll go somewhere else with you."

Is she going to follow me out of the cafeteria? I start walking to see if I got all that right. Yep, she's following me. I walk to the rotunda outside the library. We take a seat and she looks at me seriously.

"The way you left on New Year's, and you not sitting with us anymore, was that because of Harrison and Jess?" she presses again.

I should probably just pretend, be light, be all *whatever* about it. But her eyes do look concerned. "I didn't know."

"They're not together, you know. They were, yes, but she cheated with this boy ####### ######## ########### mock trial competition. Anyway it's been over for a while. They stayed friends. Except when he started liking you . . . well, I think she just got jealous. But nothing happened that night."

"I saw them kiss."

"Look, Jessica was being a flirty drunk. She downed like ####### ### ##### # before we even got there. But he wasn't into it. Harrison was looking for you everywhere. He was really bummed you weren't there."

"Okay," I say, feeling more confused than ever. So Jessica and Harrison are not together? But they were. But Frankie just said Harrison likes me? And Jessica was jealous?

"He likes you, Ana. *Likes you,* likes you," she explains, almost reading my mind. "He does. Have you not noticed him ###### ######## since we got back to school? You ######### ##### New Year's and he has no idea why."

New Year's. It all swirls together, the disappointment at realizing it wasn't the kind of date I wanted it to be, of being so overdressed. Always, everywhere, the feeling of not knowing the right words, of not fully understanding what is going on, a thrumming buzz that drowns so much out.

"They were . . ."

"I know how it must have looked to you. Honestly, but Harrison told Jess he wasn't ###### ###### as soon as you left. Seriously, Ana—he likes you. Just . . . think about it. I don't mean to get in the middle of it, but it was a misunderstanding. Really."

"I will think about it," I tell Frankie. It was nice of her to tell me all of this, but I feel more confused than ever.

To Muddy the Waters

I am not on the same page
And I got my wires crossed
And I got ahold of the wrong end of the stick
And I can't make heads or tails of so many things
here.

A country with so many phrases for
misunderstanding

Even "understand" hides itself. Under. Stand. Does
knowing something mean you have to stand under
it until it falls on you? And why is yesterday's
understanding "understood"?

TAKING FLIGHT

It's math next, so I shouldn't be surprised when I find myself walking next to Harrison in the hallway. Our arms graze as we pass and a shiver runs through me. I should say something to him. It wasn't fair how I just stopped talking to him.

"Hey," I say.

He looks at me, startled. Then his eyes light up. "Hey."

"How is math going?" I ask him. He peers into my face as if trying to figure out why I'm talking to him. I guess I'd be doing the same if I were him. I could have explained, I could have asked what was going on.

I can't even blame it on English. It was the internationally nonsensical language of boy that did me in this time.

"Not so good since my tutor gave up on me," he says. His tone is sad, his eyes squinted a little as if trying to see into the future to know how I'll respond to that. It sinks me and buoys me at the same time.

"No," I say. "Your tutor didn't give up on you."

"Seems that way," he says.

"I'm sorry. I just . . ." But no. It's too much. "I was confused," I say. "After class, we study?" I offer. I have a free today and I know he does too.

"Seriously?" he asks, his eyebrows arched, hopeful.

"Seriously," I tell him.

After class the room empties out and no one else comes in. We work on the problem set. The period goes by quickly. Too quickly. There are only a few minutes left, and I have one more formula to teach him, but this one I don't know by heart. I need the textbook. I reach in to get it, but it is scrunched in my bag, which really is too small for all the stuff I have to carry around here. I pull out my ESL notebook to make room.

"Wait, did you write this?" he asks. I look to see what Harrison is asking about. The back cover of my

ESL notebook is filled with my scribbles, ideas, notes, shards of poems, stickers, a few drawings.

His finger is pointing to one of the poems. It says:

Look my way and I am charmed
Hurt my heart and I am armed
Leave and nothing's left to do
Look your way and ache for you.

Horror swells in my throat . . . it's about him.

"No. I mean . . . yes. It's just . . . nothing. For homework . . ." I realize that's a stupid lie before I finish it. Who writes their homework on the back cover of their notebook? "Sometimes it helps me practice to try to write in English."

"This is a song?"

"Just a poem."

"That you read somewhere?"

I shake my head.

He reads it to himself and taps on the table with his thumbs. "It sounds like a song."

I shake my head again. This is so embarrassing.

He sits up, turns the notebook over like he knows I'm embarrassed he saw it.

"So . . . I have an idea. I've told you I'm in a band,

right? Could you maybe, like, write something for us? Please. We're never going to get far doing nineties ####### #######. There's not enough ###### #### ###### ## lack of lyric-writing capacity. We need you. *I* need you."

I need you. The words tingle through me like a magic spell.

My cheeks burn. I know he doesn't mean it that way, but still. I shake my head again.

"I'll pay you back when we get our record deal."

I laugh. "You would have to, if I wrote the lyrics."

"So is that a yes?" He smiles.

Finally I nod. I don't know what I'm getting myself into. But I like sitting here talking about math with him. I want to talk about more with him. "Yes."

He leans over and puts his arm around me. For months, every moment has been like the first day of school, going to the board to do the math problem when the teacher was just asking if I had the textbook. I am always worried I'm reading situations wrong. I don't know all the words.

But right now:

I am a battalion of the most delicate cranes, wings wide, flying high into the sky.

I bloom in your song
I fly through your wind
I crane hasta el cielo
When you look at me
That way.

IN PINK, BUT **NOT** SO **PRETTY**

For our movie today, Neo has brought little square bits
of pastry that look like they have skinny little strings
on top and which are jaw-achingly sweet. Baklava. We
sit in the library media room and I wonder how I'm
going to get all this stickiness off my fingers.

We're watching *Pretty in Pink*. It's about a poor girl
who likes a rich boy. She lives near some train tracks.
It seems to me that she and her father aren't all that
poor—she's got her own car and a job, so how poor
can they be? But she is an outsider in a school full of
much richer kids, so I kind of relate to her in that sense.

Also the boy she winds up with, the rich boy, reminds me of Harrison in some ways, the fresh-faced sweetness, the way his hair always seems like it needs to be cut. Except Harrison is not as clueless as the boy in the movie.

I lick the baklava off my fingers and Neo turns on the lights.

"What you say?" he asks.

"Well, I did not like her prom dress," I tell him.

"I also did not. You like the end?"

I twist my mouth to one side. I want to say more than I know how to say. "I like when love wins in the end."

He looks at me steadily. "I also like this."

I smile, glad to understand each other.

I change the subject. "The other boy, the boy who bothers her . . . . Duckie? I think today maybe would get reported, with the way he follows her around."

Neo laughs. "I think he wants to be good friend to her."

"It's possible," I tell him and smile.

"Ana?" Neo says my name like a question. His face is full of questions, actually, his eyes open and earnest and filled with a lot more than thoughts about the girl in the pink dress and the two boys who want to be with her. I look up at him. It's not like New Year's, but the look is intense in other ways. It makes me nervous about what he might say.

We never talked about the New Year's almost-kiss (if that's what it was), but I have thought a lot about it. Neo is as familiar as anything in this new world. When I'm with Neo, there is no deafening buzz, no confusion over every word. That means something.

But then there is Harrison. Harrison, the very sight of whom makes me take flight. Harrison, who Frankie said *likes me* likes me. Can I want to kiss Neo when Harrison makes me feel the way he does? I am so confused.

"I should go," I tell him, standing up. I don't know what he is going to say, but I know I don't have the right words to answer, no matter what it is, no matter what the language. "See you tomorrow, Neo."

He nods slowly. "See you tomorrow, Ana."

AÑORO

I am in the car, on the way to Harrison's house. *Harrison's house.*

We were supposed to meet for tutoring, but in math, he said, "Hey, how about we skip the math and go to my house to work on a song? My guitar is there."

I watch him while he drives. His hand on the steering wheel is distracting, just sort of casual and confident, like he was born to have his own car. He plugs in his phone and the car fills with music. It's the band I was listening to that one time. I hope it's not a coincidence. I hope he remembered and put the song on because of it.

He parks in front of his house, which is a mirror image of Altagracia's, and lets us in through a side door. He gets me a glass of orange juice and takes me to a room on the first floor. Both his parents are still at work, a discovery that makes my heart leap. He takes his guitar out from behind the couch and begins playing me a song.

He is playing me a song.

The song is beautiful, actually—simple, and a little bit sad, with a chorus with fancy finger work that sounds a little like the Spanish guitar my father used to like to listen to on Sundays at home, just guitar, no vocals. He plays perched on the armrest of the couch, one leg up holding the dark-brown, shiny guitar, the other stretched out to the floor, a tiny hole in the seam of his T-shirt at the shoulder.

When he finishes, he looks up. "It's kind of a bummer? I was listening to a lot of acoustic and there was like . . . soul . . . I was trying to get to, but . . ."

"It's beautiful," I say. "What is it about?"

"What does it sound like it's about?" He narrows his eyes a little, trying to read me.

"I heard . . . what's that thing when someone leaves?"

"Sadness?" he asks.

"No, when they're far and you want them to be close."

"Longing. Yearning," he says.

I think of the Spanish word for it, a word that, to me, seems to capture the feeling so much better than anything: añoro. And another: anhelo. But I don't tell him that.

I nod. "Yes, that's what I hear in that song." I look it up on my phone to be sure I fully understand the meaning. Too many times I think I know the word but there's something more to it. *Yearning.* I love it instantly, as close as it is to yarn, that tangled-up feeling of wanting someone or something to be near you, to be yours, and the more you try to escape the thoughts, the more they come. I am a whole ball of yearning, for home, for words. I understand this word. In some ways, I *am* this word.

He nods. He looks serious now. He slides down from the armrest and puts the guitar gently behind him.

He says, "I don't know if that's the right word. I don't always know the right words. Kind of like with math . . . it takes me a while to know how to say what I want to say." He is holding my gaze steady. "Ana, all this time that I've been asking you to help me with math, I guess what I've really wanted to say is . . ." He stops, looks hesitant.

"What?"

"What I've wanted to say is *I like you.*"

The skin of my neck blooms. I dig my thumbnail into the tip of my index finger to remember I am flesh, not just a galloping heart that's flown up to the rafters of this huge room.

"I like you too, Harrison."

"Why haven't you said anything? And why were you so weird after New Year's?" he asks.

"I didn't know . . ." I trail off. I didn't know what? I didn't know if he felt the same way? I didn't know if I misunderstood? I didn't know the rules? I think about Neo, about New Year's. I didn't know what that meant? I didn't know how I felt about it? "I . . . didn't have the words."

He leans toward me. I can feel the warmth of him. He's still looking straight in my eyes. "Is it okay if I kiss you?" he asks.

The question freezes me. Only yesterday I was thinking of Neo and if I wanted to kiss him. And now, I am looking at Harrison, and I *know* I want to kiss him. Instead of words, I use my lips. His lips are soft, and wonderful, but he doesn't move them. I get self-conscious. Am I supposed to do something more? I kiss him again. He kisses too, then pulls away.

"That was nice. I'm so happy you came over," he says.

I smile. It *was* nice. My heart is pounding. I take a breath to bring myself out of the moment.

"Hey, you want more juice?" he asks.

It takes me a beat to see how he's gone from this air-bending moment to casual, all at warp speed. But it's nice that he wants to get me juice. "Okay," I say.

He comes back with a full glass.

Then he reaches in his pocket and hands me a crane. "To keep your other one company. You still have it?"

I do, but I've never told him. After that one time he saw it, I've kept it out of sight. "I do."

This one is yellow. It's made precisely, like practice is really making perfect.

"I like that you still have it. Now, when I make them, I think of you."

He takes a breath, like he's gearing up for something. Finally, he says, "You know . . . my sister's wedding is this weekend. All these months of making cranes. I'll finally be able to show them off."

"That's great," I say.

He fidgets, shifts his weight. "I know it's last-minute, but I was wondering if . . . I was thinking maybe . . ."

I turn to look at him. He is red around the ears, on his neck.

"What?"

"I don't know. If you wanted to go?"

"Go?"

He fidgets again. "To my sister's wedding? Being as how you've been in on this crane thing from the start."

"Yes." I smile, remembering my first day of school, noticing Harrison. I could have never imagined I would be here now.

Life is strange and beautiful.

OJOS QUE NO VEN,
CORAZÓN QUE NO SIENTE

Tonight at dinner I have to look like I'm *here* though my mind is still floating above the treetops. But my father is looking at me, his eyes narrowed. I know he can very nearly smell if a boy has been near me.

"How is school?" he asks.

Safe ground.

"Good. I got a ninety-seven on my last math test."

"Why not a hundred?" he asks.

I hate this question. "Pa, it's still an A."

"And the girl? The dentist's girl?"

Even though Altagracia has many things that might have been a problem back home—the shaved hair, the makeup—here he approves of her because she speaks Spanish and her dad is a doctor of sorts.

"She's good. I'm spending the day at her house tomorrow."

He nods his approval. And then he adds, "No boys, right? You're staying focused?"

My father used to play the guitar back home. He used to be soft, and laugh, and trust. He used to sit en el patio and drink wine mixed with soda water with his brothers and cousins and the neighbors and tell stories that let me know that his teenage years were not exactly innocent. We prowl around each other now, holding up masks that get heavier every day. I don't want to lie to him, but in a way, he is lying to me, too.

"No," I tell him. "No boys."

Back home I never lied.

But everyone is different here.

THE WAY OF LIES

I tell a little white lie
That makes me feel splashed with mud
I pull the wool over my parents' eyes
And I'm itchy on the inside
I am smoke and mirrors
Afraid of the shards
I have stretched the truth
And I am a rubber band about to snap.

MY FIRST AMERICAN WEDDING

It is the day of the wedding. For once a dress is the right choice. Mine is cream, with the tiniest pink flowers. Altagracia offered her substantial closet, and I picked this simple A-line dress. And I liked her drying my hair and making some curls at the ends.

When I am ready, she spins me around to take in her work. "Divine," she says.

"I couldn't have gotten ready without you," I tell her.

She laughs. "You could have. Anyway, off you go. I've got to work on me now. I'm picking up Leticia so we can go to Green Man," she says.

I give her a hug. "What! How have you not told me?"

She waves her hand. "Eh, we'll see. I don't know what it is yet, so we'll talk about it later."

I nod. "Well, I'm happy for you." And I am. If anyone deserves to be happy, it's Altagracia.

Harrison is adorable in a suit, his tie slightly askew. I straighten it for him. The sculpture garden where his sister's wedding and reception are being held is lit up by candles in more lanterns than I've ever seen in my life, all different styles—modern and rococo, colored glass and clear. Overhead, round-bulb string lights provide a canopy, high up, giving everything a warm glow. From the string lights, more paper cranes than I would have imagined possible for any one person to make . . . if I hadn't been watching him make them all year. They're a beautiful, papery reminder that love comes in many languages and shapes, and that small things can add up to a garden full of beautiful. It's a smallish wedding, by our standards, anyway, maybe about sixty or seventy people. Guests mill about around a few rows of white foldable chairs lined up in front of a gazebo hung with flowers.

"Here, come on, let me introduce you to

everyone," says Harrison. "I'll take you behind the scenes." I nod. The ceremony is about to start, and I'm a little nervous, but I guess I've learned enough English to get by. And it's a crowd of people from everywhere—at least half the guests must be from the groom's side—so I am not the only one for whom English is a second language.

He walks us behind a tall stone gate and up a path to a glass-enclosed room. Inside, his sister is easy to spot, not because she's the only one in white— actually, her dress is a simple knee-length sheath that hardly looks different from a guest's. No, the way you know she's the bride is because she looks happier than anyone I've ever seen.

"Molly, this is Ana," says Harrison. She looks like him, but with a heart-shaped face and a wider smile. Her hair is up in a simple twist. Up close she looks even happier than she did from far away.

"Congratulations," I say.

She gives me a hug. "It's so nice to meet you," she says. "Thank you for coming." She turns to Harrison. "Have you seen Tak? You should meet Tak," she says to me.

"Stop trying to play hostess and relax. I'll introduce her to your wonderful husband."

She gleams. "Not yet. Which reminds me. You should go sit. We saved seats for you in the first row. You know how Mom gets. ######### ######### ##### #########."

He hugs her. "Don't worry. You look amazing. You're not going to run away, are you?"

She laughs and swats him.

We go sit. Harrison's hand is warm in mine. This is my first wedding in the United States, and I realize it looks both nothing and everything like I might have imagined. It's quirky, it's unique, a mix of cultures and languages. On the other side, I can hear the groom's family speaking in Japanese. The vocalist is singing a song in a language I can't make out. And, yet, the joy in the air is something you can feel, beyond words, bigger than any one language can contain. Harrison's mom and dad, who have made their way to our row, give a quick wave. I wave back. They look so happy too.

For some strange reason, although it doesn't look like the wedding in *Sixteen Candles* at all, the scene from that movie comes up in my mind. I remember sitting in the library with Neo, the way he noticed the same things I noticed, even before we talked about it. I wonder what he would say if he were here.

The ceremony begins. Tak looks nervous, and

happy too, in a slim-cut blue suit that's a shade darker than those of his groomsmen. The bridesmaids are all in hues of cream, but in all different dresses. I've never seen that either, and I like it. The officiant is a tall, regal woman in a plain black dress. Nothing marks her as a clergyperson, and I wonder if she is.

They get to the vows. Molly is turned half away from us, since we're sitting on her side, but I can hear her voice clearly.

"Takumi, my love, this day is finally here. ######## ######### #####." Soft laughter from the crowd. "Because you always know how to cut to the heart of things. You always know how to speak the truth. I love the way you can always make me breathe when I'm talking too fast, when I'm nervous. I love the way you can always get across the busiest street. ########## ########## ########. Takumi, I am so proud to become your wife, because you make me a better me. Because I trust you. Because you help me trust me."

I close my eyes. In my heart there's . . . recognition? Yearning? *Añoro*. I wonder what it's like to be seen that way. To have someone see the thing that makes you you, and love you for them. For your you-ness to be the thing that's perfect for one special someone. It sits in my throat like a violin holding a note.

"Molly, I too am beyond elated that our day has arrived." His accent is crisp, vaguely British. "####### ######## ######## ##########. I love you for the way you slip your hair behind your ear when you read. For how kind you are to every small creature, even when you don't know anyone is looking. For how you're always the first one to dance, even if there's no music playing, and you're never afraid of sounding terrible at karaoke."

"Hey!" She laughs.

His face gets serious again. "I love that every word, every story, every moment I experience, the first thing I think is about how much I want to tell you about it. I love the way you quicken my pulse. The way you challenge me. The way stilling you stills me. I love that of all the days written in the book of life, I don't think one could be more perfect than this one."

A tear falls out of one of my eyes, softly, slowly.

Harrison looks at me and smiles. His hand is still warm in mine. I swap out my other one. If he notices the tear, he doesn't point it out.

THE THINGS UNSAID

Tak was not kidding when he said Molly is the first one on the dance floor. People were still finishing up their dinner and she was already grooving to some beat only she could hear. They didn't do the whole "first dance" thing, instead inviting everyone out onto the dance floor all at once. The band is quirky too, not what I would normally think of as dance music. But we've danced like crazy anyway. And now Harrison and I have gone through a walk along a winding footpath lit by tiny fairy lights.

"That was a nice ceremony, right?" he says.

"I loved it," I say truthfully. "The vows were beautiful."

He studies me, like he's been thinking about something and I may have some clue he needs. "Ana, I love the way you roll the *rr*'s in my name. I like the way you can always figure out a math problem, like you've got some kind of calculator in your brain."

I swat him, and he smiles.

"Now you," he says.

"I . . ." Maybe it's the emotion of the ceremony, or how he put me on the spot, but I can't think of anything. I like Harrison. Of course I do. But as I play back what Molly and Tak said, everything that comes up for me about him feels so . . . silly. I like him because he looks like a boy in a Netflix movie? Because he folds cranes for his sister? Because he has a nice voice?

"I . . . ," I say again.

He laughs and puts his arm around me. "Don't worry. It was just some dumb idea."

I stand up and take his hand. "Come on, let's go dance."

THE THINGS SAID

Today is a winter day that wants to be a spring day. The warmish breeze feels good on my face. We are having ESL class outside where we ate the McDonald's food all those months ago. I like that Mr. T. does this—has class in different places, does unusual things. Besides the fact that he makes school interesting, moving outside gives me a break I don't always get in the day.

On the walk out here, I get a text from Harrison. He says he's busy with family stuff after school today but he'll make it up to me with a fire chai from Green Man. I send him back a thumbs-up. The whole wedding was so romantic . . . but I couldn't get our conversation about the vows out of my mind. Why couldn't I think of anything to say? Was it just the pressure of the moment, or did it mean something more?

Neo glances over at me. I should tell him about Harrison, that we're dating now, but for some reason, I can't. Ever since our stilted conversation in the library the other day, it feels like there's been some unspoken thing between us. What did he want to tell me before I cut him off? Did I want to hear it? Do I want to hear it now? I'm tired of all the not-knowing.

Mr. T. walks over, a huge grin on his face. "I have an announcement!" he says.

He pulls out a rolled-up magazine from his back pocket. The cover is matte, a beautiful picture of vibrantly colored street art. He looks in the table of contents, flips to a page.

He holds it in front of me. Then he holds it up to the class. "Ana submitted one of her poems in English to a magazine competition . . . and she won! They printed it!"

There it is: My poem. *My name.*

"It just came this morning," Mr. T. says. "Congratulations, Ana."

I run my finger over my name. My name, printed here by these strangers, to be seen by people I don't know. I can hardly believe the joy. It's like being seen, in the best way. I wasn't sure I wanted to enter because I didn't want the pain of *no*, but I can barely contain the joy of *yes*.

"Would you like to read it to the class?" Mr. T. says.

My face blushes. Writing a poem is one thing, but performing it is another. I shake my head.

Mr. T. smiles. "Maybe another time."

The class claps. Neo gives a whoop. I feel something akin to dizzy, but much, much better. Mr. T. is beaming at me.

"Congratulations," Neo says, his eyes glowing. "I am so proud of you."

I am so proud of me, too.

A THOUSAND SHIPS

After school, Neo convinces me to go totally off plan and watch a movie not made in the eighties, and not at all the type of movie Mr. T. has recommended: the movie *Troy*, with Brad Pitt. I suspect maybe he just wanted a break from all the talking in movies. *Troy* is a movie you can understand if you don't speak a word of any language. It's really just about the battle scenes.

"This is very famous Greek story," he tells me during one of the talking parts we're ignoring.

"*The Iliad*," I say.

"You know!" he says.

"Of course," I say. "Everyone knows *The Iliad*."

"Oh, Paris and Helen. The things that love can make you do," he says.

I turn back to the screen. Two men who both seem like they're Brad Pitt are sword fighting next to a pristine blue sea.

"You know what amazes me most about *The Iliad*?" I ask him.

"What?" he says.

"Not just *The Iliad*, but the Bible, and *The Odyssey*, and all those stories from a long time ago. Even though now we think of them as being written down, they started as stories that people told each other."

"Huh," he says. "I didn't know that."

I remember how I felt about reciting my poem. "I wish I could do that. Share my words out loud."

Neo is completely ignoring the screen now, watching me intently, his eyes alive with something I can't read.

He nods. "The most important words are the ones we're brave enough to share."

WHAT'S THE BIG IDEA

The next day, Neo finds me at my locker.

"I have an idea!" he says.

"What?" I ask.

"When we were watching *Troy*, and talking about poems being spoken, I started to think about how people still do that today. Poetry slams, they're called? I look up this word, 'slam,' and it makes no sense. But people say poems out loud."

"I've heard of that. I saw an old movie that they did that in. I would love to see one in person."

He stands up straighter. "You see one!"

"What do you mean?"

He shows me his phone. It's a picture of a woman with big, beautiful hair standing on a low stage, talking into a microphone, her arms out wide.

"Where is this?" I ask. I can't imagine it's in town and I haven't heard about it. Mr. T. would have told me for sure.

"New York City," says Neo.

"Oh," I say. It might as well be on the moon. For all the months we've lived here, and it being only an hour and a half away, I still haven't been to New York.

"We go," he says. "And you will perform in the poetry slam."

I am filled with panic. "What? No."

"Yes!" Neo says. "Ana, you have the words. Now you must share them."

I think about it. Can I really recite my poetry in front of strangers? What if they think it's terrible? What if I'm booed off the stage?

But what if it's the best feeling in the world?

"My father would never let me." He grumbles about it sometimes, los Nueva Yores, he calls it when he's being especially negative about it, the land of mayhem and probably a little bit of depravity. He's a driver, but he turns down trips that would take him to New York, preferring his reliable Newark Airport runs. He says it's because the traffic is too bad, but I don't totally believe him. I guess I understand some of his nerves about it. It looks overwhelming in movies, those massive crowds, the yellow taxis always almost killing people when they step off a curb, or splashing muddy rain on them. But that scariness is laced through with something else, something electric. I so want to see it.

"I know it's important to be good son." He corrects himself, "Daughter. But it is also important to do the things we love. I'll go with you. Come on. We go, we come right back."

He seems so alive and happy. And I feel alive and happy too, that he listened to the things I said the other day, that it made him think, that he's done all this research. But most of all, it feels like a big, terrifying, wonderful step.

I nod. "I'm in," I say.

LOS NUEVA YORES

I board the bus behind Neo, heart pounding. I've never done anything like this before. All night I tried to come up with a way to tell my parents about the trip that wouldn't make them explode. Finally, I took the chicken way out and told them I was going to Altagracia's for the day. I feel bad, but they didn't even let me go into el centro by myself back home, and today . . . Today I needed to go to New York.

New York City!

Land of Carrie Bradshaw and Rachel Green, of subways and Central Park. I've worn what I hope is an outfit appropriate both to New York and a poetry slam:

a black T-shirt with a cropped red satin baseball-style jacket over it, black jeans torn at the knees, and black ankle boots. I paid special attention to making big waves in my hair. Neo looks like he also tried to pick a New York outfit: a charcoal-gray button-down and slim, dark jeans. Instead of his usual sneakers, he's in dark-red leather ones. His hair is combed neatly, and he obviously shaved this morning. He smells like aftershave, and there's a little nick on his jaw where he cut himself.

Finally, we rumble out of the other side of the tunnel, and the bus drives into a giant, grimy building. I jump down every step of the bus and onto the cement sidewalk. I wait for Neo to get off and I throw my arms around him, jumping up and down. "We are in New York, Neo!"

"It smells terrible." He wrinkles up his nose.

"It's that bus. Let's get away from it."

We find our way to the stairs and take them down two by two, then get to an escalator. We scoot around the people who are just standing on it listlessly: a woman with four overstuffed shopping bags, a guy with face tattoos, an ancient-looking grandma we're careful not to bump. How can they all look so bored? Don't they know they're in New York?

At the foot of the escalator, I spot light from the street in the distance, and I say to Neo, "C'mon," and take off in a run. We run past coffee shops and a drug store, and burst through the black-framed glass doors onto a street, under an overhang. There's a random statue of a fat guy looking very pleased with himself to the right. I run up to the curb, dodging people on the teeming sidewalk, trying to get to the sun. There, across the street, as if it knows I need a sign that I'm really, really here, a glass building winks in the sun. *The New York Times*, it says.

Neo is beside me. I give him a hug of gratitude. I wouldn't be here if he hadn't suggested it. How have I stayed away this long? How did I not insist we come here on the very first day? The yellow cabs jockey for position, and the sidewalk is crammed with what looks like a thousand people. A light turns, and there's honking, insistent and annoyed, and the river of life proceeds, pedestrians jumping in front of cars like they don't even see them, one guy pounding on the hood of a car that dared to inch forward.

New York!

"Where do we go?" I ask Neo.

"Well, the poetry thing starts in two hours, so we have some time," he says.

"I want to see everything." I say.

"Okay. Let's just walk around here for a little bit first."

We go to the corner and wait for the light. As soon as it turns green, people start moving in a giant sea of bodies. And it's not just the number of people, but the many different kinds. It's like they decided to take representatives from every size, gender, shape, color, and nationality and put them all on one city block. To our left, a couple is arguing in what sounds like French. In front of us, some guys have their phone out and are looking at the map and pointing in different directions as they speak a language I can't even begin to identify. When we get to the other side, we walk past a table covered in folded-up scarves.

I look at Neo, to see if he's noticing this too, the great mix of everything. We're walking past a store with a giant window filled with every fabric ever created, in every color that has ever existed. It's a little like New York, in store form.

"This place is amazing," he says.

We stumble into a giant intersection that looks familiar to me. It's got massive screens, like television screens, but building-sized, and it's even crazier than the place outside the bus terminal, if that's possible. There are even more people here, some standing around and looking up, or taking pictures, kids on shoulders, people with noses in phones. Here, truly everyone seems to be speaking a different language. The stores are bigger, louder, brighter. A trumpet player belts out a beautiful song. There's a dude in his underwear and a cowboy hat, and nothing else. SpongeBob SquarePants is taking pictures with a string of gleeful small children.

"Times Square," says Neo, looking at his phone.

Of course. The place where the ball drops on New Year's. It is huge, bigger than it looked on TV. I love everything about it instantly, its carnival atmosphere, its brash, in-your-face attitude, its multitude of languages and voices. It's like New York making a show of being New York.

"Let's take a picture with SpongeBob," I say. So we do. We drop a dollar in a bucket he has at his feet.

After going into a bunch of stores, we make our way in the general direction of the poetry slam. The thrumming, frenetic life of Times Square gives way to narrower streets, although in any other place in the world, these streets would still be mind-blowing. It's like energy radiates off the sidewalk, from the scent of nuts from the vendors on street corners, to the shouts of people trying to entice you into stores, to the colors and textures on the thousands of things for sale in every kind of store imaginable, to the sound of music wafting out of cars. My body soaks it all up, thrilling with it, vibrating at its frequency.

"I think it's here," says Neo. Much too soon. He's been looking at the map to navigate us, but I've been looking at mine to google a thousand questions that have popped up at every step. How many residents in New York City? How many tourists each year? How many flowers in the thousands of planters? What used to be there before Times Square? I've learned a thousand things, and shared all of them with Neo happily. But, still, that means that when we get to Twentieth Street where the poetry slam is, it surprises me.

I peer inside. It's a small café, dark, with tiny wooden tables and black walls. My heart thumps.

Neo puts his hand on my elbow. "Come on. It's going to be awesome. Let's go inside."

So we do. The woman at the front points us to the back, behind a partition. That's where all the people are sitting, maybe about twenty-five, arrayed around tables like the ones out front. It's dark here, lit up by a lamp in the corner. A guy with a fancy mustache greets us. "Are you here to listen or to speak?"

I say "listen" and Neo says "speak" at the same time.

The guy with the twirled-up mustache gives us a "which is it" look.

Neo points to me. "She's speaking," he says. My throat tightens up. Last night I pulled out the poem I had written for the literary magazine, and read and reread it to memorize it, but my shoulders feel a little quivery, like I'm going to explode in trembles. The man gives me a clipboard to write down my name on a list.

The first person to get up is a girl with silver and blue hair, who does a poem about the power of being a girl. The next is about a heartbreak, the one after that about the heavy expectations of parents. They're good, so good, much better than I can be, at least today, with my accent and my inexperience. But somehow, instead of being intimidating, it's uplifting, like I've just come over a ridge and seen clear to a faraway horizon I didn't know existed.

Finally, it's my turn. Neo gives my hand a squeeze. I stand up. I shuffle my feet, like maybe I'm a battery that can be charged by contact with the earth. Or this floor, really. I get to the microphone and look at the faces of the people there. But it's too much, so I focus on Neo. He smiles and nods, a "you got this" look on his face.

I take a breath. I begin. "It's called 'An Old Story with a New Ending.'"

"America, I long for you.
I long for the day I don't translate you in my head.
For the day I am not "other" by the way I form your
words.
I want to write notes in the margins of you and so
say something new about you
That's never been said before.
I want to fold you into squares and put you in my
pocket
And let your confidence work on me like an
enchantment.
I want to run my finger on the length of you,
California to New York,
I want to grow to your size, scale you, surf you.
I want to be enough for you, and have you be the
thing that tops me up like a bottle in which the water
overflows.
I want to learn your melodies, the discordant and the
sweet,
I want to tell your tales, and change their endings
So that they include a girl like me
Who longs for you
You tip your hat and say, 'You belong here.'"

The crowd claps. There is something heady in this welcoming sound from strangers. I smile and look over at Neo again, my heart pounding, feeling the power of telling a story to strangers, the way people have felt for thousands of years. Here, around our version of the campfire, I have told my tale, and I've been heard, and the power of that is thrilling. I wonder if just one little bit of the feelings I shared will carry with at least one of these people. I hope so.

I let go of the mic and walk back to where Neo and I are sitting. He leans into my ear and says, "I am so glad I know you."

I smile. I don't know why, but his words make my eyes fill up with tears, with the emotion of the moment. "I am so glad I know you too," I say.

EMPIRE STATE OF **MIND**

"Okay, one more thing," says Neo, when we're outside.
"You ready?"

I nod. I'm high from the rush of saying my poem,
of people coming up to me at the end and saying nice
things.

We walk a few blocks and suddenly we're in front
of a massive building.

"What is this?" I ask.

"The Empire State Building." He smiles.

"What!" I say.

You can't see the top from the street. It's huge and

hulking. "Come on," he says. "I got us tickets to the top. You want to go up?"

I can't believe it. Can't believe that he knew how much this would mean to me, can't believe that he planned all this, can't believe I'm finally going to go.

I make it through the line and up the scary-fast elevator in a fog. Dreaming of this is one thing. Being here is surreal.

We get out of the elevator and step onto the observation deck. It looks like the whole world is laid out all around us, far below us, bustling and massive, millions of people in thousands of buildings, the heartbeat of the whole world.

"Do you like it?" he asks.

I turn to him. His eyes are studying me.

"I can't believe you did this. It's amazing."

He smiles wide. It's startling and it warms the spot around my ears, and I look at him—really look at him. In a rush, my mind is flooded with words. Words that describe all the things I love about Neo. Words that I couldn't think of with Harrison. *Neo, I love how you capture the essence of a building in a sketch, the soul of what makes it beautiful. I love how you always look at me like what I have to say is important. I love how you always make sure there are enough snacks. I love that when you read my words, they matter to you. I love how you feel like home.*

Neo looks into my eyes too. The moment expands a little, explosions in my ears, the glow from the Empire State Building playing off his eyes, already so blue on their own.

"This has been a perfect day," he says.

I lean in closer, just a centimeter, just a bit, because the crackle of the moment makes me do it, because he looks so perfect with his charcoal button-down and the dimple in his chin. Because he made this whole, magical day possible, the trip to the place I've most wanted to see, the moment up on the stage, and now, here, this beautiful view, sparkly and perfect and almost more than I can soak in, like it's a moment I want to be bigger for, but which I'm perfect for, both at the same time.

He leans in. When his lips touch mine, the moment shivers through me, his lips, warm and perfect, part mine. His hand is on the small of my back, and he pulls me in, and I can't breathe, but I don't want to, because all I want to do is kiss this boy in the most perfect spot on the planet. I lean against him, and he puts his arm around me to pull me even closer. I move my hand up to his jaw, then back toward his hair. I run my fingers through it.

He pulls back and looks in my eyes. "I've been wanting to do that for a long time."

I rest my head on his chest. I can't believe this just happened. It's amazing. And . . . it's complicated. Because . . . Harrison. But I can't worry about that now. I want to soak in the perfection of this moment. I will have to tell Harrison what this means. But not right now.

I put my thumbs in his belt loops and look at him again. I want nothing more than for him to kiss me again. Or maybe I'll kiss him.

His phone buzzes.

"Hey, is that your phone?" I ask.

"Yeah. It's been going crazy."

"You should check it," I say. I hate to have the moment broken. But maybe his dad needs him or something.

Which reminds me, I haven't checked my phone for a while either. I slip my phone out of my back pocket. Dead.

When I look up at Neo, his eyes are worried. "That's Altagracia. Your dad is trying to find you."

THE WORST CALL EVER

My throat is thick with a big ball of panic. This is not good. I run a thousand things through my head. But there really is only one thing to do. Call my dad.

This is going to be bad.

Neo offers his phone. I take it, and dial my dad's number. He made me memorize it, even though I told him that was dumb because I had it stored in my phone. But I guess it's for moments like these that it's good to know a number by heart.

"Hello?" he says, his voice hot and fast.

"Papi, soy yo."

"¿Qué número es este?"

"I'm on a friend's phone," I say. Factual. Incomplete but factual.

"What friend? And don't tell me Altagracia because I already know that's a lie. It was not good of you to put your friend in a situation where she had to lie."

"I'm sorry, Pa," I say.

"Which friend?" he pushes.

"My friend Neo. From ESL."

"¿Qué clase de nombre es . . ." He catches himself. "What kind of name is Neo?"

I furrow my brow. "Greek?" I say. Is that what he wants to know?

"No. Boy or girl?" he asks.

I look up at Neo. He looks worried, maybe a little guilty. "Boy," I say.

My father curses in Spanish under his breath a bit. It sounds like he's pulled the phone away from his mouth. I hear my mother's soothing tones telling him not to worry, that at least they heard from me and I'm okay.

He puts the phone back to his ear. "Tell me where you are right this minute and be waiting for me outside. I am on my way."

"Actually, Pa, no. It's going to take me . . . . it's going to be a little while before I can get there."

"Where are you?" He sounds furious, a pot on a fire that's too high.

So I tell him. And that's when he really gets mad.

THE FALLOUT

I walk into the apartment building with a terrible dread. I'm not sure how I get up to the third floor, but suddenly I'm there.

I open the door.

My father is standing in the doorway to the kitchen, a few steps away from the door. My mother clasps a sweater tight around her behind him.

He storms up to me.

"What were you thinking?" he snarls. "Who was that boy?"

Every tightly wound expectation and warning in my father has suddenly unraveled, and he's screaming.

I don't think he's ever yelled this way at me before. There was one time when I went to the store but got distracted with friends playing jump rope, back home. He was livid that day. But I could tell, even then, that the anger was about worry.

This anger doesn't look like it's about worry. It's about fury.

"¡Te hice una pregunta!" He's screaming in Spanish. He has totally forgotten his own rule. Do I answer in Spanish or English? What will make him less mad?

"I went to . . . there was a place where you recite poetry. I wanted to go," I say. It's no use lying. I'm tired of it anyway.

"With some boy we've never met? What are you thinking? Do you know what boys think of girls who lie to their parents just to run off to . . ." I have never seen his face so red. The lying isn't just lying. It's lying about a boy.

My mother puts a birdlike hand on his upper arm. "Mi amor, if we just . . ."

He screams over her. "No, none of this. Is this what you want for her? She's going to run the streets now? ¡To los Nueva Yores! ¡Así, sin permiso! With some boy who didn't have the respect to come ask for her at home, properly?"

The idea of Neo coming up here for the seventeenth-century ritual of having to ask my dad permission to take me out mortifies me beyond measure.

"It's not like that here, Pa!"

"It's like that *here*, in this house! This is *my* house, and it's like I say it is! And do you know what could have happened to you over there? In a city with millions of people, and with us not knowing where you were? And you without your phone?"

"I had my phone. It just died."

I open my mouth to say something else but my mother shakes her head, a warning to stay quiet.

"Mi amor, please, keep your voice down," she says to him.

He lowers it to a growl. "Who does that? Lie like that? Run off with some boy? You're like these Americans."

He means it as an insult, and that cuts deepest of all. What does he want from me, anyway? He wants perfect grades, he wants me to love the topic he thinks is best, he wants me to stick to old rules about boys like we're living in the Dark Ages. And he wants me American but not too American, brave but not too brave. Just as suddenly, I am the one yelling.

"That's what you wanted!" I say. "*No Spanish*, you said. *Learn American ways*, you said! You wanted an American daughter. Well, you got one."

I storm past him to my room and throw myself on the bed. I want to move the bureau in front of the door so that no one can ever come in here again. I want to crawl out the window. I want to scream. I want to play music loud enough to wake up the whole block.

He follows me to my room. "Your phone, right now."

This winds me. How can he take away my phone? "It's dead," I say. Like that's going to make a difference.

"Right now," he says.

I pull it out of my back pocket and give it to him, a seething fury crawling up my body. At least there's one good thing: after I hand him my phone, he leaves me alone.

NEITHER HERE NOR THERE

I bury my face in my pillow. It smells stale, like every-thing in this dimly lit, grungy place. We weren't rich at home, but we weren't like here. The frustration bub-bles in me and tears come. They're not sad, though, they're boxed-in, angry tears. They're trapped tears. Nothing will ever be like before we came here. I punch the pillow. I wish I could scream until all this frustra-tion and rage evaporated away.

There's a soft knock on the door. I turn on my back. "What?"

My mother peeks her head in. "¿Puedo entrar?"

I nod.

She sits on the bed. She's so thin now, so frail-looking. I wonder where the woman from back home has gone. I haven't seen her laugh since . . . since when? I can't remember.

She moves my hair away from my forehead. "Remember when you were little?" she asks. "I . . . I had . . . how do you call it? Superpowers. You wouldn't let anyone hold you but me."

I don't say anything.

"One 'Arrorró mi nena' and all your problems would be solved."

In a sudden, irrational thought, I almost want to ask her to sing it again, the lullaby she sang me when I was little. But then that idea fills me with a dark swirl of anger and sadness. It plays in my head, swelling up my throat. It definitely wouldn't help.

"It doesn't work that way anymore," I tell her.

"I know, m'hijita. I know. But it's all going to be okay. You'll see. He was just so afraid," she says. "That wasn't the best way to tell you, but we're alone here, with no family. And if something happened to you . . ."

She thaws me, a little. "I know it was wrong to lie. But would he have ever let me go?"

She looks off at the wall. "No, probablemente no."

"And how could he yell like that? He was never like that back home."

She puts her hand on mine. "No," she says. "He is different. But aren't you? Aren't we all different here? I was able to see you grow. He left a little girl and now has to get used to you being almost a woman. It's like learning to live with strangers. Not just you, but me."

I don't want her to stay, but I don't love when she leaves, either. I lay back on my pillow. Tonight is literally the worst night for me to be without a phone. I can't be this girl, the one who is going out with one guy but kissing a different one. Home or here, I don't want to be that person.

I close my eyes. The sight that comes to me is Neo, eyes full of reflected light, about to lean in to kiss me. The sensation of the kiss shivers through me, the mix of all the things that happened today.

THINGS THAT HAPPEN
AT LOCKERS

Monday morning hangs on me like a wet rag. This weekend things at my house were miserable, and today I have to talk to Harrison, which does not help my mood. I have to tell him what happened. What I did.

I get to school early, because I want to get out of my house, and because my father insists on driving me. He doesn't say a word the whole ride. I turn down the hallway where my locker is so I can put my afternoon books in it before finding my way to class.

There are people lingering around it. I squint my eyes to see what's going on. It's early, and there's

280

usually not random people just standing in front of it. Except, no, it's not random people.

It's Neo and Harrison.

My heart drops. I consider running in the other direction, maybe actually running off to New York. But, no, Harrison sees me, and Neo follows his gaze to see what he's looking at. There's only one thing to do. I make the rest of the endless walk to my locker, my joints feeling loose as jelly.

"What's this?" Harrison asks, his face stone. I look at where he's pointing. There's a single two-toned pink rose sticking out of my locker.

"I don't . . ." I trail off. I look at Neo. His face is one of confusion, maybe a bit of embarrassment.

"I wanted to surprise you. Because of . . ." He doesn't finish the sentence.

"What's going on?" asks Harrison.

"I . . . Harrison, I wanted to talk to you today."

"I've been texting you," says Harrison.

"I'm sorry," I say. "My dad took away my phone. I got in trouble."

"Because of New York?" asks Neo.

"What about New York?" asks Harrison.

I can't do this.

"Neo and I went to New York on Saturday," I say. "My dad is mad."

"You and Neo went to New York? And now you're leaving my girlfriend flowers?" he asks Neo. "Not cool, dude."

Neo's eyes flash with anger. "This is true?" he asks me. "This is your boyfriend?"

"Neo, I'm sorry, I wanted to tell you, but . . ."

"Wait, you're sorry about what?" asks Harrison.

I take a deep breath. "Neo and I . . . . we went as friends, but while we were in New York, something happened."

"Something?" asks Neo bitterly.

"We kissed, Harrison. I'm sorry. I didn't mean to hurt you . . ."

Harrison's jaw clenches. He looks so mad.

Neo takes the flower out of my locker. "I didn't know you had a boyfriend." He turns to Harrison. "No disrespect," he says, and walks off. He tosses the flower into a garbage can.

I have said everything all wrong. I wanted to explain to Harrison that I've been feeling weird since the wedding, but I didn't want it to be like this, so embarrassing, so hurtful. And I said all the wrong things about Neo, too, making what happened sound smaller than it was. It wasn't just something. It was a thing that was right, like shining a light in the dark and finding what you are looking for. But that was impossible to say in front of Harrison, and now Neo's walked off and I can't explain.

"I really liked you," says Harrison. He turns and walks away. My eyes sting and my throat tightens.

I walk through the day in a rough fog, every word I said at the locker spinning in my head. If only I'd asked to speak to each of them privately. If only I'd talked to Harrison after the wedding, explained how I was feeling right away. If only I'd talked to Neo about all this on the long bus ride home. I could have explained. Maybe. He would have understood. He has listened and been with me, and there's no reason for not telling him the truth.

I am not like this. I am not this girl.

I have to talk to both of them. I'll find Neo after ESL, and I'll explain. I want him to know it was not just some moment that I got swept up in, but an instant of seeing clearly something I hadn't known before. As I replay all our afternoons, our movie nights, our easy laughs, the way he always asked to read my poems, how he found the place where he just knew I'd be able to share something that mattered, it looks so obvious now.

But I don't get to tell Neo these things at ESL, because he doesn't show up.

I walk the halls between classes looking for him, but he's nowhere to be found. I do see Harrison, but he doesn't want to talk to me. Even Altagracia is home with a cold, so I can't talk to her about what a mess I've made. I end the day completely wiped out. And now all that's left to do is go home to the dingy apartment where my parents are furious at me.

At the final bell, I step out toward the parking lot. The day is sleet gray, like even the sky wants to be unfriendly. Suddenly, I see a blur, someone sprinting. Then someone else. Then someone screams, "Hey, come on!" A deep voice shouts, "Go back to where you came from!"

I take a step back. There's a group forming near the door where I just came out, a cluster of people.

I run to the tangle of bodies.

I push my way through the crowd. I have a sick feeling that I need to see, although I don't know why. At the center is a blur. Two people, I think. One has the other in a headlock. They are swinging widely. It's all blurry, voices, grunts. A voice I recognize.

Neo.

It's Neo in the headlock, swinging his arms,

connecting with a thud on the other boy's lower back. He pulls Neo tighter.

The other one is the guy from the hall, the one with the crew cut and the stupid comments, the one who tried to knock the meatballs out of Neo's hands the day of the potluck.

I jump into the circle. "Hey! Stop! Stop!"

Neo wrestles free from the headlock and jumps on the other guy. He has blood on his face.

"Neo, stop! He's not worth it! Stop." I try to grab his arm, pull him away. The other guy shoves my left shoulder, throwing me off-balance.

Then all at once there are teachers, a gym teacher and some other ones I don't recognize, and Neo and the other guy are being pulled away. I run after them.

"Hey, he didn't do anything," I say to the gym teacher, pointing to Neo. "It's not his fault."

"They'll figure this out in the office," says the gym guy. He's big, and square, and isn't looking at me.

I stop, my heart thumping sickeningly. I have to tell them Neo didn't do anything. That he wouldn't. I have to make sure he is okay.

I run to the door where they went in.

UPSIDE-DOWN CAKE

They don't let me in to see Neo at the office. They don't even let me sit inside. I sit outside on a bench where people line up for late passes in the morning. The minutes tick by in what feels like an eternity.

Finally, the door to the office swings open. The other boy walks out. He gives me a dirty look but, luckily, doesn't say anything. It's several more minutes before the door swings open again.

It's Neo. I spring up. He has a cut on his cheek, but it's stopped bleeding. He'll have a moretón there tomorrow. Black and blue, as they call it in English. And the cut may scar.

"Neo, are you okay?"

It takes him a minute to focus his gaze on me, like someone trying to figure out where a dangerous noise is coming from. "Ana. What are you doing here?"

"I had to make sure you were okay."

He shoves his hands in the front pockets of his jeans and starts walking toward the door. "You shouldn't have waited," he says.

I catch up to him. "Hey, come on. What happened?"

"It doesn't matter."

"Neo, please talk to me."

"That stupid kid has been telling me . . . It doesn't matter."

"Please. What?"

"Just ugly things. Threatening me. Like every time he sees me outside ESL. And why does he have a problem with me, anyway? I never do anything to him."

"So don't worry about him."

He shakes his head. We're at the door to the outside. He leans his shoulder into it. He winces but pushes it open. "No," he says.

"What do you mean, no?" I step outside behind him.

"I mean no, it's not worth it. I thought I could do something here. But . . . no. I'm done."

"Done how? I don't understand." I jump in front of him to block his path. He stops walking.

"I mean I'm done with this school. With this country. Nothing is the way I wanted." He looks off to the distance, then back to my face. His eyes aren't crystal as usual, but cloudy, like the day.

"What? No," I say. "You're just mad." He can't possibly mean what it sounds like he's saying.

"They suspended me. I tried to explain he jumped on top of me. I tried to explain all the things he says. But they didn't listen."

I want to hug him.

Neo continues. "This place is for some people. Maybe you too. But not me. I'm going home."

Home?

"What do you mean? Home to your apartment? Come on, I'll walk with you," I say.

"No," he says. "To my country. To my people. I'm going to Cyprus."

How can he want to go home? After he's worked so hard? After we both have? I feel my heart is sinking to the ground. I feel like it is beating outside my body.

"Neo, please. You're mad now. I'll come to your place after school. How long are you suspended?"

"It doesn't matter, Ana. I have been fighting here for a long time. I want to go home."

"Neo, will you please wait a minute? I'm so sorry about before. And now this happened and I know it's not the time to talk about it, but you're saying these things about going home, so I just want you to know. I'm sorry about this morning. I'm sorry I didn't say anything to you. And then we kissed and I . . . I should have told you about Harrison, but then my dad was mad and I didn't know how. If I had known earlier how you felt, I would have done things differently."

He stares at me. Finally he says, "No, Ana. You knew how I felt about you. You've known it since New Year's. And you knew what you felt about me. But you wanted your American boyfriend. Well, what is that saying Mr. T. says? You can't have your cake and eat it too."

He walks past me and starts in the direction of his place. The set in his shoulders makes it pretty obvious he doesn't want me to follow. I stand and watch him getting smaller and smaller, until he turns right past the chain-link fence around the soccer field and disappears from view.

There's nothing left but to go home. I take the walk

slowly, Neo's words rattling in my brain. That saying that used to make no sense: have your cake and eat it too. I get it now. It's about not wanting to choose, even when you have to.

Take off the helmet and put on a mask
Breathe in the air
That filters through me
To walk
Through this world
With the right face
Descarada—
Like I don't want to be.
Faceless—
The old me stripped away.
A girl I don't recognize
In my place.
I want to turn my face to the sun
And be all of me in one place.

AMIGA DE VERDAD

When I get home, I sneak my phone back and text Altagracia about what happened. She writes back that she's coming over. Even though I am still grounded, my mom says it is okay. I think she can tell that I need my friend.

Altagracia comes up. Her face is bare, her hair bunched at her crown, and she's in a jogging suit.

I meet her at the door and walk her to my room. My mom says a quick hi and goes out to the market. My dad is working. I feel a little lighter knowing it's just Altagracia and me in our apartment.

"Are you okay?" I ask her. I don't think I've ever seen her with no makeup on before.

"Letting my pores breathe." She fans her face and laughs, her dimples pronounced. She looks so very young without her usual face on. "But you look awful, no offense."

I take a breath.

"Okay, tell me everything," she says, getting serious.

"Ugh. Everything's a mess, Altagracia. Everything. My dad is still so mad at me. And Neo told me he's moving back to his country."

"What? Because of the fight with that Neanderthal? I heard about that. He's not worth that."

"I don't know. That, but other things too." I look at her guiltily. "I kissed Neo."

She raises her eyebrows at me. "Oh," she says.

"Yes. That was not a good thing to do."

She looks at me. "Can I tell you something? And stop me if you think I'm off base."

"Of course." I have to think for a moment what *off base* means, but then I remember it's about baseball, how you are only safe if your foot is on the base.

"Ever since you told me you liked Harrison, I tried

to see it, you know? And even though you seemed into it, there was something missing. Honestly, I think you liked the *idea* of Harrison more than you ever liked the *reality* of Harrison."

I let this sink in. Maybe she is right. Why did I like Harrison, after all? Because he looked like the boys from the movies? Because everything seems so easy and American with him? He is everything I thought I wanted—and that stopped me from seeing the real thing right in front of me.

I take a deep breath in. I hadn't imagined it was this complicated. Isn't love supposed to be something you just know, like running after someone in a prom dress, or kissing a boy over a birthday cake?

"You said I was brave for going out there, for trying. But I hurt two people who didn't deserve to be hurt. I disappointed my parents. I scared them. And Neo said this thing, that I wanted to have my cake and eat it too."

She sprawls backward on my bedspread made of patches of blue-and-gold bohemian fabric that my mother stitched together on an old Singer. She says, "Girl, cake tastes good. You made a mistake. It doesn't make you a bad person. What you do after, that's what shows who you are. I'm a big believer that things happen the way they're supposed to, even when they hurt. Like you coming here, and us becoming friends. I'm better because I know you."

I smile. She's going to make me cry if she keeps this up. I hug her. "I'm better because I know you too," I say.

She breaks the hug, raises her eyebrow mischievously. "Damn straight you are. Look at how on point your eyebrow game is right now."

I throw my head back and laugh.

She leans in conspiratorially. "Now let me tell you what happened with Letitia."

"What?" I ask.

"We kissed."

"What?!"

"I know. And let me tell you, I could kiss her for days. I finally get it." I soak in every little detail. It makes me so happy to see her this overjoyed.

THE HARD CONVERSATION

I have thought a lot about what Altagracia said, about how it's what we do after mistakes that shows who we are. I want to be the kind of person who does the right thing after making mistakes.

"Thank you for talking to me, Harrison," I say. My heart is thumping. We're sitting in the rotunda. It's lunchtime, but it's quiet. He's in a green hoodie and jeans. He still looks like always—scrubbed and bright-eyed, full of certainty that the world is good. But there's something else, too, a guardedness. It hurts my heart to think I had something to do with that look.

We sit down after brief hellos. "So what's up?" he says. Not unkindly, but not friendly, either.

I take a deep breath. There are many ways not to have the right words. "I'm . . . I just wanted to tell you I'm sorry. You were sweet to me. And I made a mistake. You didn't deserve that."

He looks away. "It was shitty to find out like that. With some other dude putting a flower on your locker."

"I know. I messed up. Things were kind of up in the air with us and it just happened. Not that those are good excuses. You deserved better."

He's quiet. "You were the first girl I liked that much in a long time. That way," he says, finally. His face looks pained.

His words smash over me, like a wave that takes your feet out from under you. "I should have done better," I say. "I really am sorry."

"You liked him the whole time?" he says.

"It wasn't like that. I really thought . . . honestly, I thought for a long time that what I liked about him was that he knew what it was like to be from somewhere else. It took me a months to realize it was something else. I wish this relationship stuff came with instructions."

He laughs sadly. "Yeah."

"Can I give you a hug?" I ask. "Would that be okay?"

He nods, and I hug him. It's quick, and chaste, but it feels like the start of forgiveness.

Suddenly there's not much more to say. "Goodbye, Harrison," I say, standing up. "Thank you for listening."

He scrunches his mouth in a sad smile. "Goodbye, Ana," he says. He leaves in the direction of the cafeteria. I go the other way.

When you walk in the sun and think it is honest
When you step off a curb and think it is kind
When the words in your throat flutter off in the
silence
When the people you love turn their heads as you
whisper
When the world seems indifferent to all that you say
When you think you are heard but all is confusion
Then you tip your head up to the blue and you ask it
Will it ever be right or will it always be so?
Will I ever feel sure like the Earth on its axis?
Or is meaning always lost in a tangle of sky?

THE LAST DAY OF
THE BRAIN JOCK REBEL

I would give anything not to be at this party, but there's nowhere I would rather be, either. Mr. T. has organized a goodbye party for Neo. It's been days since I've seen him. He hasn't been in school because of his suspension. He hasn't been answering any of my texts. I can't believe that it's over. I can't believe that he won't let me explain. But if I was in his shoes, would I? Probably not.

I look over at him. Neo seems sad, but something else, too, a mixture of resigned and relieved. That probably hurts most of all. I am only now beginning to understand just how much I thought we were in this together, learning how to make our way through the bramble of this foreign land. But now he is leaving, and I've never felt more alone.

Mr. T. clinks a plastic fork on a red Solo cup. "Okay, listen up, people. I've put together a little video of Neo's time here. So everybody, take a moment."

A video? He turns off the lights and turns on the smartboard. It's black. Then it fades to a picture of us on the first day. When did he take that picture? I don't even remember. Outside his car holding up McDonald's bags. A video of Neo holding empanadas and doing the "tips of the fingers to the lips/yummy" sign. A picture of one of Neo's drawings of a skyscraper, the detail exquisite, almost like metal lace. A long shot of us playing soccer on the grass. I had totally forgotten that moment. A picture of him all bundled up in the snow. A shot of the back of our heads through the window in the library media room. I squint and I see the TV, with a shot of *Pretty in Pink* when Duckie is driving his bike past Andie's house in the rain. When did Mr. T. get all these pictures?

I want to cry so much it hurts my throat.

Thankfully, the video is short. Neo's eyes are a little glassy too.

"Neo, you've been an important part of this class,

and I hope you remember your American adventure fondly," Mr. T. says.

"I will remember with much fond," says Neo with a sad smile.

"Okay, everyone, how about we go around the room and tell Neo one thing we appreciated #### him. I'll start. Neo, I appreciate you giving your all to the work. You are a cool kid."

Bhagatveer says, "I appreciate you helping me understand the homework sometimes."

"I like how you draw."

"I like that ride you gave me on your scooter."

"I am grateful for the way you stood up for me when that boy was picking on me."

"Ana?" says Mr. T. when it's my turn.

"I . . . there's a lot," I say. Mr. T. nods gives me time to figure out what to say. "You always had the best snacks for our movie watching." Neo studies me. His eyebrows look just the slightest bit disappointed, a formal cast to his face, like he's holding himself back from me. Or like he thinks that's what I'm doing with him.

Mr. T. laughs. "The way to a girl's heart is through her stomach."

I've never heard this saying, and it grosses me out a little, but I think I understand what it means. It reminds me of my grandmother. Barriga llena, corazón contento.

There is more I want to say, but not here, not in front of everyone.

The bell rings. Everyone clusters around Neo to give him a hug. I hang back. I want to be the last one.

Finally, when it's just us, we walk to the door. "I have something for you," I say. I pull it out of my bag. It's a T-shirt that says

Brain
Jock
Rebel
Recluse
Princess

There's a hint of a smile on his face. "The 'princess' will be a little hard to explain back home," he says. "Thank you."

"When do you leave?"

"Tomorrow night."

We're at the door of the classroom now.

"Neo, I've been trying to text you."

"I know. I don't know what to say."

"But *I* know what to say."

303

"It's all in the past."

"It doesn't have to be."

He shakes his head. "Ana, I am grateful for all those movies and all that . . ." He drifts off. He looks uncomfortable, like he's trying to hold himself in tightly, not say too much. "Anyway, I have to go now."

"I can walk with you," I say.

He shakes his head again, then looks off like he's thinking about something.

"I have to go," he says. He gives me a kiss on the cheek, sweet, soft, sad. Then he walks away. I turn in the direction of my locker before the tears that are threatening to escape fall out of my eyes.

When I turn back around, he's already gone.

I before E except after C
Or when used in "ay"
As "you light up my day."
Also except as in "weird"
And "albeit"
And "forfeit"
And "fancier"
In a language full of exceptions to the rule
I should have seen the exception that is you.

THE THINGS THAT CALL YOU HOME

Scrape.

Tink.

Chew.

Dinner with my parents is excruciating now. I wonder if my dad is really just going to be mad at me forever. I eye the clock. Neo's flight is tonight. In his small apartment that already lacked any sign of hominess, every last thing is being put in a suitcase or in a box by the curb, and nothing will be left of him, not his sketchbook with the beautiful buildings, not that charcoal button-down he wore to New York, nothing.

My father is hunched over his plate, angrily

shoveling food in his mouth. My dad of back home would find this dad rude.

Then again, a lot of things about my dad have changed.

My mother clears her throat. "Your father and I were talking," she says.

I look at her. She has her head cocked at him in the "well?" position.

He sits straighter. "Yes, we were," he says. He chews for a long time, longer than anyone ever has to chew anything. Finally he takes a deep inhale and says, "I am sorry I yelled."

I study his face. I've heard him apologize to my mom, but never to me. That's not how fathers are where we're from.

He goes on. "When I came to this country first, I knew why I came. But I didn't know how it would knock me down to be without you and your mother. I felt so much responsibility. I had to find the right town for us. I had to learn the language as fast as I could. I had to figure out how things worked here, how to protect you. But here I was most nights, just weighed down by so much loneliness. Just wondering if we had done the right thing. But then you were here, and you were practically a woman, and you seemed so distant and . . . well, I don't know you anymore, it is true. I pushed, I know. I was stubborn. But you were stubborn too, of course." He smiles.

I smile back.

He goes on. "All this is to say, I don't know all the answers. I don't know if I've done the right things. But everything I've done, I've done for you." He puts his hand on mine. "Estoy tan orgulloso de ti. You must know that, right? You're learning English so much faster than I ever could. You are a poet. You are my greatest joy, Ana."

A tear spills out of my mother's eye. She looks relieved, and something else. My father even looks a little misty. He gets up and I stand up too. My mother reaches her arm around us. We haven't hugged like this, all three of us, in so long. Not since we got here. My father kisses my hair.

The tears that come are sweet.

"I'm sorry too," I say. "I shouldn't have lied. I won't do it again. But sometimes I just didn't know how to tell you things, or ask you things. I'm not the little girl you left behind." This line I say directly to my father. My mother was there the whole time. But for him, I was one person, then I was a different one.

"I know," he says softly.

I give him another hug. For the first time in a long time, it feels like it always used to.

"But there's something more," my mom says, a statement, not a question. She could always reads the currents of me, like I'm a boat map and she's an old mariner.

"That boy," I say. "Neo."

"You had a fight?" my dad asks. "He was a jerk? Because if he was . . ."

I shake my head. "No. I was the one." I tell them everything: Harrison, the fight, Neo getting suspended unfairly. I even tell them about the kiss and the awful moment by my locker. To their credit, they keep their faces even, although this is a lot for them to take in.

My father inhales deeply, lets out a sigh. "You really aren't a little girl anymore," he says wistfully.

I smile. "I've been trying to tell you."

He nods. "Okay, well, then I'll do my best to tell you what I think without imagining you in pigtails. This boy, the one who is leaving, he means a lot to you?"

I nod.

My dad puts his hand on my wrist. "No te preocupes, m'hijita. If it is meant to be, it will be."

I laugh. "You're not one to talk about fate much."

He takes another deep breath. "Did I ever tell you I was in a band once? We played cafés in Buenos Aires, in Rosario, in Mar del Plata, spent a summer down by the lakes. I was going to be a singer, you know? The things you think about when you're young."

This is such a strange thing to learn about my dad, like he once lived on another planet. I guess I've seen pictures of him with a guitar, and I've heard him play, but I never knew it was something he did. Something he dreamed of.

"And then . . ." He smiles at my mother. "There was a girl I'd left back home. And I went back. I wasn't sure if she'd wait for me, but she had. And I decided home and family were more important than whatever I was chasing in cafés and dance halls. And then you were on the way and I knew there was a different life for me."

I can't tell if he's happy about this or not. Or whether this is in response to my comment about fate. Maybe this is a story about taking the wrong path.

"How do you know?" I ask. "How do you know what the right path is before you take it? What if in another life you could have been a famous singer, but you gave all that up for just this?"

"There's nothing 'just' about this, nena. But, can I tell you what? I got quiet one night, and looked at the stars, and it was like I could hear your mother's voice asking me to come home. So I did. And what I learned was: some things call you home." With that, my dad gets up from the table and goes into the other room. When he comes back, he's holding a small package wrapped in tissue paper. "This was outside the door today. It's for you." He hands it to me.

It feels like a book. I hold the bundle to my heart, give my dad a quick hug. "I'm going to sit outside for a little while, okay?"

My dad smiles. "Sí," he says.

THE GLOSSARY OF HAPPINESS

I sit on the bench in front of the apartment building. I turn up my face to the sky. It is an orangey blue. The moon is massive and alive, and it seems to want to say something to me. Neo is probably on his way back to Cyprus now. *Come back to me*, I whisper. The sky beams down wordlessly, embarrassed for me, I think. Some wishes are too big even for the moon.

I take the tissue-paper-covered notebook in my hands. It's tied with cream-colored twine. I unlace the knot and pull back the pink tissue paper. Inside is a small wire-bound notebook. It's got a little window cut out of it, and through the window I can see, stenciled like an architectural drawing, the words "The Glossary of Happiness."

I turn to the first page. It says, "Joyous: how I feel when you smile."

The tears sting almost at once.

I go back to the first page. Inside, there's a piece of lined loose-leaf paper folded in four. I unfold it. It says:

Dear Ana,

All this year I've been thinking a lot about words. About how we all feel the same things, all over the world. About how we all find our own words to say the things we feel. I looked at how hard you worked to collect every single word. How that day at the poetry slam you let them out of you, like a piece of you being spoken.

When I started this notebook, I never meant to give it to you. But when I went to pack it, I realized I would regret it if I didn't tell you. This notebook would never have happened if I hadn't known you. Every time I wrote in it, I was writing about you. I couldn't leave without telling you all that.

Ana, leaving makes me sad for a lot of reasons,

but most of all because I didn't say all the things I could have said when they could have made a difference. But a lot of those things are in this book.

I hope you are happy. I hope you learn every word you want to learn and speak every one you want to say.

Goodbye, Ana. I hope you have a beautiful life.

Neo

I thumb through the book. Page after page of words. There are definitions and jokes and observations. All the words we talked about that have no definition in any other language: gezellig, in Dutch, like the English "cozy," but not quite. And a bunch of the Spanish words I told him I couldn't find English words for, like trasnochar and sobremesa, the word he liked so much that day in ESL class. I read them all, then read them again.

The book makes me sad, but full of hope, I realize. I want to find my voice, and that's about more than just memorizing all the right words.

I close my eyes and think about what my father said at dinner. I get quiet, and look at the stars, and ask them what the right path is.

Dear Neo,

Thank you for the notebook. I am sorry for the things I didn't say, and sorry for the things I didn't hear.

I have been thinking a lot about words too, but now that you're gone, so many of them sting. Movies. Dragon. The Empire State Building. Because words aren't really just sounds scribbled down. They are the whole thing that they stand for. Collecting words is collecting little bits of life.

I hope you've landed safely. I hope it's okay to email you every once in a while. I know you may not want to hear from me, but I want to try, Neo. I miss you already.

Love,

Ana

Dear Neo,

I hope you've settled in back home. Your family must be happy to see you. Things here are different without you. But some things are good, like that kid who bullied you got expelled. I wish he would have gotten expelled for what he did to you instead of the other fight he picked the week after they let him come back to school, but I guess we can call it karma, as they say here. Altagracia is dating Leticia (remember I told you about her? From art class?) now and she seems so happy. Valentina finally came to visit, and she and Altagracia got along so well! My parents went to a party at the social club, and they got all dressed up, and my mother came back looking happier than she has since we've been here. It's funny, trying to find the balance between where you're from and where you are now. I'm beginning to wonder if I won't always be a little from both places.

What about you? Will you forget your time here and go back to being from there?

Or, maybe, can you find your way back here? I hope it with my whole heart, even if it is too much to hope.

Love,
Ana

Dear Neo,
I haven't heard back from you, but I'm writing anyway. I don't want to give up. I miss you so much.

I know I may never see you again. And maybe my dad is right when he says things happen as they should. Maybe you were meant to help me find my way here, learning along with me. Even if that's the only thing we were supposed to be, you made a big difference in my life.

In some ways, things are good here. I tested out of ESL for next year. And I talked to Mr. T. about the poetry slam in the city, and he agreed to be the adviser for a new poetry club at school. I'm hoping we can have two big slams a year.

I hate how things ended between us. I've been thinking a lot about another word: regret. I wish I could do it all different, Neo.

Love,

Ana

Dear Neo,
I miss you.
Love,
Ana

Dear Ana,

I'm sorry I haven't written. I haven't known what to say.

I too feel regret.

I too miss you.

I made my decision to come back home too quickly. Home. What does home mean, anyway?

It came to me last night when I was looking at the stars and wondering if you saw the same stars.

Ana, I think maybe you are my home, too.

My application for college is due in the fall. The English I learned will make my TOEFL easier. I have found an architecture program in New York that I hope I can get into.

If I do, will you meet me at the top of the Empire State Building?

It will be a while, but I want to make up a new word, just for you and me, something that means: worth waiting for.

Love,

Neo

ONE YEAR LATER

I spot him from far away, but he's looking around, his eyes scanning the crowd. The wind is strong and my hair is flying everywhere. But then . . . we're on top of the world. Of course it gets windy up here.

I offered to meet him at the airport. But he said he'd meet me here, at the Empire State Building observatory. Like the first time. Like a new first for us.

He looks a year different. His hair is a little shorter. He is deeply tanned. He is more muscular than last year, too. I'm nervous. I smooth the front of my dress. Will he still feel the way he did last year? I know that with every note I've gotten from him, my feelings have only grown.

But then he spots me and quickens the pace. And his arms around me tell me everything I was hoping to know.

I put my face in his shoulder. I feel his breath in my hair.

"Agapimu," he says, squeezing tighter, letting out a sigh it feels like he's been holding in a long time. I know what it means because he told me once, and later I doodled it in my notebook and tingled at the knowledge, even though he hadn't meant it about me. I say it back to him.

"Mi amor," I whisper, smiling up at him like the sun.

AUTHOR'S NOTE

I have spent a lot of time thinking about writing a book on not speaking English . . . in English. I once spoke no English. I came to the US undocumented and sat in many a classroom like Ana, wondering what was going on. Like Ana, I marinated in abject humiliation after I missed a word or a social cue. It's been a long time, but I remember it vividly. When I decided I wanted to tell Ana's story, I understood I'd be doing two things: explaining the experience of not speaking English but doing it as the person I am now, English speaker of many decades, lover of Shakespeare and Flannery O'Connor, English major, book nerd. And also, realistically, I am a writer in the United States. And many of my readers speak English, although, of course, it would be my honor for readers of other languages to find their way to it as well.

As a reader, I imagine I might have had the question: Is the story told in retrospect by Ana after she speaks English? Or is it translated? The simple answer is I want *you* to decide. I want you to create that part of the story. It is yours. It's also occurred to me that, even to Spanish speakers, some of the words or conjugations in this book might look different from the ones you know. There are many variations to the language, and the one I learned uses "vos" instead of "tú." So when you run across something quirky, I hope you'll smile and realize that all languages have their idiosyncrasies.

There are words we hear in our world, see in our books. But they are just tools. Behind them all, there is the experience of being ourselves. That experience has no language, no issues of logic. This is a story of wanting to find yourself, of feeling excluded, or worrying whether you're enough. It is also about how the people we meet and love and need on the journey mean everything. There is no language and every language for that.

I took four years of high school Italian, which means when I travel to Italy I can order my food in decent Italian (unfortunately, 87 percent of waiters respond in English). I once loved a man from Cyprus, so I used to be able to talk to his family in passable Greek. When my mother comes over every Sunday to drink mate (that's "mah-teh" to English speakers), I speak almost exclusively in Spanish, even though we both speak English. My mother sang me lullabies in Spanish, but I sang to my own children in English, the (main) language of my beloved adopted land, save for one secret lullaby I did sing to them in Spanish.

We find many ways to say the things we feel. But what's important is not what separates us, or the particulars of how you say a thing or how I do. What's important is that in our similarly beating hearts, love sounds like love without any words.

ACKNOWLEDGMENTS

If you are like me and enjoy reading acknowledgments pages, you may have caught on to the same trend I have: authors often feel the need to express amazement at just how big a group of people it takes to make a book and to support one writer's dreams. I am no different. I'm close enough to the start of my writing career to remember the fantasy of the lone, brilliant soul at the old typewriter, the writer I aspired to be. The reality is more like this: one lone, often-muddled soul firing off emails and making calls to ask a thousand different questions, request support, plea for coffee dates wherein plot points can be discussed and literary wounds nursed with swigs of mango dragon-fruit lemonades and espresso. There is nothing solitary about it (in fact, it really can't be done solo) and I am so grateful for that.

I've also studied acknowledgments pages and tried to figure out what the order of mention means. I'll spare you the effort here: everyone on these pages is important and magical. That my brain came up with one name over another in any particular order is an accident of synapses that bears no inherent meaning. And, also, if you know you've helped me on my way and I've somehow neglected to mention you, chalk it up to those synapses firing a bit more slowly than they once did.

First, to the fantastic crew of writing friends who never tire of discussing All the Things, from craft to the best stickers to use as rewards on my calendar: you are a lifeline. From the SPA people who helped me see the bigger picture, to my writing group: Ismée Williams, Betsy Voreacos, Hannah Lee Jarvis, Lisa Hansen, and GG Collins, who never get bored of pointing out my blind spots, although you'd figure I'd have learned by now. To my sparkle ******* on Slack, Pat McCaw, Gina Carey, Gail Wilson, Tashi Saheb-Ettaba, Timanda Wertz, David Daniel, and Jamieson Haverkampf. To

Anne Ursu, Laura Ruby, and Christine Heppermann, for being everything I want to be when I grow up, and to the Highlights Foundation for the comfy cabin and the loft. To Tracy Banghart, without whom none of this would have happened. And to the brilliant and ever-patient Yvonne Ventresca, writer extraordinaire and dear friend, a thousand years of good luck to you for being the tortoise to my hare, a perspective that this fidgety rabbit needs in the extreme. I am grateful for you every day.

To the Alloy team, a heart full of gratitude. To Viana Siniscalchi for the endless patience, to Sara Shandler for always knowing the right thing to say and for running a meeting like a boss, to Josh Bank for the wit and the photo with Wonder Woman, to Joelle Hobeika for the keen eye, and to Josephine McKenna for being all-around awesome.

To the Harper team: Alessandra Balzer, for teaching me that dreams really do come true and that cat pictures are best when shared, to Caitlin Johnson for the keen eagle eye, to Jackie Burke, Cindy Hamilton, Sabrina Abballe, Shannon Cox, Patty Rosati, Katie Dutton, Mimi Rankin, Andrea Pappenheimer, Kerry Moynagh, Kathy Faber, Megan Gendell, and Jon

Howard for helping Ana find her way to readers, and for every other awesome human at Balzer + Bray and HarperCollins who touched this book. A special thank you to Jenna Stempel-Lobell, Rude, and Maja Tomljanovic for the gorgeous cover art.

To Sara Crowe, superagent among agents, and to everyone at Pippin, including Holly, Elena, Cameron, and Ashley: all the doughnuts to you.

To my brother, Pablo, for his shared love of story (esto sí va a terminar bien) and his wife, Daniela, for striving to make the world a bit more beautiful each day. To la Mami for those many long days in the basement apartment teaching me that squiggles could be made into words, and words spun into stories, and for keeping books around even under the hardest of circumstances (and for the spelling checks on this book). And to my children, Andreanna and Zachary, who came along and made everything make sense, like magic. (Which, of course, you are.) Thank you for being awesome every day and for understanding when dinner stinks because Momma's got a chapter to finish.

And to you, reader. You hold in your hands something that for many years I didn't imagine a girl like me would have a hand in creating, and which you made possible. If gratitude could be spun into sparkles, I'd sprinkle you with thousands of them so everyone could see you shine for the dream maker you are.